Kiss of Death

That night Brandt lay in the darkness, waiting for sleep.

He stared at the ceiling, listening.

Silence.

So why did he have this strange feeling, the feeling that something was hovering nearby? Something dangerous.

He glanced at the clock. I've *got* to get some sleep, he thought.

He closed his eyes.

A soft whisper of cold air rippled across his skin.

He opened his eyes.

Another puff of cold air. Like an icy breath.

And then he felt the brush of lips on the back of his neck. Cold, cold lips.

Books by R. L. Stine

Fear Street

THE NEW GIRL
THE SURPRISE PARTY
THE OVERNIGHT
MISSING
THE WRONG NUMBER
THE SLEEPWALKER
HAUNTED
HALLOWEEN PARTY
THE STEPSISTER
SKI WEEKEND
THE FIRE GAME
LIGHTS OUT
THE SECRET BEDROOM
THE KNIFE
PROM QUEEN
FIRST DATE
THE BEST FRIEND
THE CHEATER
SUNBURN
THE NEW BOY
THE DARE
BAD DREAMS
DOUBLE DATE
THE THRILL CLUB
ONE EVIL SUMMER

Fear Street Super Chiller

PARTY SUMMER
SILENT NIGHT
GOODNIGHT KISS
BROKEN HEARTS
SILENT NIGHT 2
THE DEAD LIFEGUARD

The Fear Street Saga

THE BETRAYAL
THE SECRET
THE BURNING

Fear Street Cheerleaders

THE FIRST EVIL
THE SECOND EVIL
THE THIRD EVIL

99 Fear Street: The House of Evil

THE FIRST HORROR
THE SECOND HORROR

Other Novels

HOW I BROKE UP WITH ERNIE
PHONE CALLS
CURTAINS
BROKEN DATE

Available from ARCHWAY Paperbacks

99 FEAR STREET: THE HOUSE OF EVIL
R·L·STINE

The Second Horror

A Parachute Press Book

AN ARCHWAY PAPERBACK
Published by POCKET BOOKS
New York   London   Toronto   Sydney   Tokyo   Singapore

AN ARCHWAY PAPERBACK *Original*

An Archway Paperback published by
POCKET BOOKS, a division of Simon & Schuster Inc.
1230 Avenue of the Americas, New York, NY 10020

ISBN: 0-671-88563-4

First Archway Paperback printing September 1994

10 9 8 7 6 5 4 3

FEAR STREET is a registered trademark of Parachute Press, Inc.

AN ARCHWAY PAPERBACK and colophon are registered trademarks of Simon & Schuster Inc.

Cover art by Bill Schmidt

Printed in the U.S.A.

IL 7+

The
Second Horror

Prologue

The ghost of Cally Frasier peered out of an attic window. A shadow floating in shadows, she stared down at the front yard and watched as the new family started to move into the house.

My house, Cally thought.

99 Fear Street.

The house where I lived. And where I died.

"You will be sorry," Cally's ghost murmured bitterly. "I promise you will be sorry."

No one heard Cally's bitter promise. That didn't matter.

She would make it come true.

Watching the new family, a teenage boy and his parents, Cally thought of her own family.

Gone. Vanished.

They abandoned me here, Cally thought without sadness. Her anger didn't allow for sadness.

The evil drove them away.

As she had every day since they'd left, Cally thought about the house, the house that had become her tomb.

The house was built over thirty years ago, she knew. Built on cursed land.

The first owners never moved in. The man who built the house brought his family to see it, and left them alone for five minutes.

Five minutes.

When he returned, his wife and children were dead. Their heads ripped from their bodies.

He hanged himself one month later.

Here. In this house.

For thirty years, no one would live here.

Then my family moved in—and became victims of the evil.

My little brother James. And his puppy. Lost forever. Lost somewhere in the walls of this house.

My father, blinded by a thick cloud of evil.

My mother and Kody. Kody, my twin sister.

All driven away by the evil.

But I'm still here, the ghost of Cally thought. The evil would not let me go.

The evil is inside me.

I feel it running through me, night and day.

Cally tossed back her head and let out an angry wail of frustration. Then she returned to the window.

The strangers were invading.

A big van was parked in the driveway. Movers carried carton after carton into the empty house.

The husband and wife stood watching with their

arms around each other. Then they opened the trunk of their car and began to unload cartons—oddly shaped boxes marked FRAGILE.

Their teenage son stood nearby, holding a black and white cat. The boy was tall and good-looking.

When she was alive, Cally might have liked him. She might have thought he was cute.

But now she was dead. And he was alive.

They couldn't even be friends.

Could they?

The shadow of Cally slipped and slid among the house's dark shadows. She glared down at the new family.

Come in, she urged them silently.

Come in. I'm waiting for you here.

I'm ready to welcome you to 99 Fear Street. I have a welcome I don't think you will forget.

Chapter 1

"Hey—be careful with those boxes!"
Mr. McCloy shouted.

Brandt McCloy watched his father chase after one of the movers, who had four large cardboard boxes piled in his arms. The top box teetered, and Mr. McCloy caught it as it fell.

"Those are priceless tribal masks," Mr. McCloy scolded the mover. "They're very old!"

"Sorry about that," the mover replied, hurrying inside. Brandt thought he didn't sound sorry at all.

Brandt stroked Ezra, his black and white cat, and sighed. "Dad and his masks," he murmured to Ezra. "He probably thinks if one breaks, it means seven years bad luck."

Ezra purred in reply.

Brandt stared wistfully at the family's new house.

A new beginning, he thought. A whole new life.

The house stood two and a half stories tall. Its gray shingles were chipped and stained. The old trees surrounding the house cast it in deep shadow.

It might have been nice once, Brandt thought, noticing two window shutters hanging from their hinges. But it sure needs help now.

Five steps led to a small, sagging front porch. The front door was surrounded by cracked stained-glass windows that badly needed to be replaced.

The house is so run-down, Brandt thought. But his parents thought they'd be comfortable there.

Brandt hoped so.

He was darkly handsome, with wavy black hair hanging loose, framing his face and flashing brown eyes. He wore faded jeans and a shirt made from colorful handwoven cloth.

A small leather pouch hung on a leather string around his neck. This he never took off.

Brandt turned as Mr. McCloy stormed out of the house, scowling. Mrs. McCloy trailed after him.

"There are rats in there!" he cried angrily. "In the basement!"

Rats, Brandt thought unhappily, petting Ezra. That's all we need.

"No problem, Dad," he said. "There's got to be an exterminator in town."

"I checked this house completely before I bought it," Mr. McCloy fumed. "There was no sign of rats in the basement two months ago."

"You must have missed them somehow, John," Mrs. McCloy said. "It's not the end of the world."

"I'm calling that real estate agent and demanding

that he get over here and do something about this. What was his name again? Lurie?"

"Lurie?" A man's voice interrupted. It seemed to come from nowhere. "Did I hear the name Lurie?"

Brandt and his parents turned toward the voice.

A young man stood on the sidewalk, smiling at them. His hair was straight and black, and he had a black mustache. He wore gray denim overalls and carried a tool kit.

"Don't mean to interrupt," the man said. "I just happened to overhear—"

"Do you know him?" Mr. McCloy asked. "Do you know Mr. Lurie?"

"I've heard of him," the man answered. "The people who used to live here . . . I heard them mention the name."

He held out a long-fingered hand. Mr. McCloy shook it.

The man introduced himself as Glen Hankers. "I do odd jobs, handiwork, that sort of thing."

"Great," Brandt's father said. "I'm John McCloy. This is my wife, Barbara, and my son, Brandt. You know anything about rats, Mr. Hankers?"

Hankers nodded. "Pest control is my specialty. Why don't I take a look?"

Mr. McCloy gratefully led Mr. Hankers inside.

Brandt glanced at the movers, who were still hauling boxes into the house. "Will you take Ezra for a while?" he asked his mother. He held the cat out to her. "I think the movers could use some help."

Mrs. McCloy frowned. "I wish you wouldn't,

7

Brandt. You've got to be careful. Your condition—"

Brandt sighed. His mother was always worrying about him. "No problem. Nothing too heavy," he said, impatiently pressing the cat into her arms. "Don't worry so much."

Mrs. McCloy's frown deepened, but she took the cat. Brandt rubbed the small scar on his left cheek. Then he made his way to the moving van and carried a small carton of books into the house.

After two or three trips, he heard his father calling to him from the living room. "Hey, Brandt. I could use some help in here."

Brandt set a box of books on the floor of the hall and walked into the living room.

"Mr. Hankers says he can get rid of the rats in no time," Mr. McCloy said. "I guess I overreacted a bit."

Brandt's father sat on the living room floor among a dozen cardboard boxes, carefully unwrapping his tribal relics. One by one, he peeled away the newspaper wrappers to reveal ancient spears and delicately carved, boldly painted masks, most of them twisted into frightened or cruel expressions.

Next he pulled out reed pipes that had been used for blowing darts. The darts were made of silver and honed to razor-sharp points.

"I want to get these things up on the wall before we do anything else," Brandt's father said. "It will guarantee we'll have good luck in our new home."

"You don't really believe that, do you, Dad?" Brandt asked, opening one of the boxes.

"You never know, Brandt," his father answered. "It can't hurt, can it?"

"I guess not," Brandt replied.

He heard his mother walk into the house and pick up the box of books he'd left on the floor. Ezra wandered into the room and rubbed against Brandt's leg.

Mr. McCloy nailed a hook into the wall. Brandt held up a spear. It was long and straight, with a sharp bronze point.

Brandt's father stepped aside as Brandt began to hang the spear on the hook.

Suddenly Brandt felt a sharp tug. "Hey—what's happening?"

The spear seemed to jump out of his hand. Point down, it plunged to the floor.

A yowl of pain shattered the silence.

Brandt gazed down—and cried out in horror.

"Ezra!" he screamed.

Chapter 2

The cat uttered a feeble groan. The spear had pierced all the way through his furry body. Bright red blood puddled onto the floor.

Its eyes wild, the cat frantically squirmed and jerked. But it couldn't free itself.

"Ezra!" Brandt dropped onto his knees beside the twitching cat.

"Don't touch him, Brandt," his father instructed. "Get the phone. Try to reach a vet."

His heart in his throat, Brandt raced for the telephone.

"At least Ezra didn't suffer too long," Mr. McCloy assured them at the dinner table that evening. "The vet said the pain probably lasted only a few seconds."

"And Ezra was getting old, Brandt," his mother added. "He wouldn't have lived more than a year or two longer anyway."

Brandt nodded. He knew Ezra was old and would have died soon. But to die so violently . . .

He could still picture the cat with the spear in its side.

What a way to start out in our new house, Brandt thought unhappily. Some new beginning.

He shook his head as if to clear the thoughts away.

His mother set a paper plate in front of him. A slice of pizza. He picked it up and bit into it.

"Pizza—what a treat!" Mr. McCloy exclaimed through a mouthful. "I don't think I've had pizza in two years. Has it been that long, Brandt?"

"I had a slice two weeks ago in the airport," Brandt replied. "On the way home from Mapolo."

His mother laughed. "You couldn't wait to get your hands on pizza the whole time we lived on the island. You whined and complained about not having pizza every day."

"*Anything* would've been better than that taro mush!" Brandt exclaimed.

"Do you think the grocery stores are open on Sunday?" Mrs. McCloy asked.

"Probably," her husband answered. "Nothing closes in the states anymore."

"Then I'll go to the store tomorrow and buy some *healthy* food," Mrs. McCloy announced, biting into her pizza.

"Is that a threat?" Brandt joked.

"Come on, Brandt," his mother said. "You know you like healthy foods. Why, you were eating like a native by the time we left. You *asked* me to make stewed mushrooms and coconut for your birthday, remember? And don't you miss the pineapples?"

Brandt remembered how sweet and juicy the pineapples were on Mapolo. Maybe he did miss the island a bit.

Brandt had spent most of his life traveling to exotic places with his parents. For the last couple of years they'd lived on a tiny, remote island in the Pacific called Mapolo, where Mr. McCloy, an anthropologist, studied ritual magic.

"Are you looking forward to school on Monday, Brandt?" Mrs. McCloy asked as she handed him a glass of Pepsi. "Nervous?"

It was the middle of October. Brandt hadn't been to school yet.

"Why should I be nervous?" he replied. "After Mapolo, high school should be a breeze."

"I think you'll enjoy it," Mr. McCloy said, wiping cheese off his chin with a paper napkin. "Your mother was right—you *do* need a couple of years of normal American life after all the traveling we've done."

"And if you don't like it," Mrs. McCloy suggested, "think of it as another anthropology project. The rituals of American high school students!"

Everyone laughed.

When the time came to leave Mapolo, Mrs. McCloy said she wanted Brandt to live in America for a few years, and Mr. McCloy agreed. He accepted a teaching post at Waynesbridge Junior College—and moved the family to nearby Shadyside, where the high school was considered more challenging.

"Remember that old woman?" Mrs. McCloy asked. "What was her name?"

"Zina," Brandt replied.

"Right. Zina. Remember that day she disappeared? The whole island searched for her. But her daughter kept insisting Zina had turned into a panther."

"And she wanted *me* to trap the panther," Brandt remembered. "I never understood that. Why me? I was just a fourteen-year-old kid."

"Because of the prophesy," Brandt's father explained. "The village sorcerer said something about a young stranger coming to the island—a young stranger who could break the spell on Zina. And you were the only young stranger around."

"I always thought that girl made the prophesy story up," Brandt's mother said. "I think she had a crush on you, Brandt."

"Mom—she was twenty years old. I was only fourteen. There's no way she had a crush on me!"

"You never know, Brandt," Mrs. McCloy teased. "Different cultures and everything—"

"Anyway," Mr. McCloy cut in, "it's nice to live in a real house again. I won't miss our leaky old leaf hut."

"Even with rats in the basement?" Brandt asked.

Mr. McCloy didn't reply. Mrs. McCloy said brightly, "Of course, the house needs work. It's always that way when you move. We'll just think of it as a project—a family project to work on together."

Brandt rolled his eyes. Sometimes his mother was so chipper, it made him sick.

"And we'll get a new cat, Brandt—if you want one," Mr. McCloy offered.

"I'm not sure I do," Brandt said. "Not yet."

"Well, think about it," Mr. McCloy said.

Brandt closed his eyes and saw Ezra, pinned through the back with the spear.

"Yeah, I'll think about it. Thanks, Dad," he said quietly.

Brandt rolled over in bed. Ezra usually slept beside him. Instinctively, Brandt reached out to pet him. His hand landed on the cool cotton sheet.

I can't believe the poor guy is dead, Brandt thought.

He lay in the dark, listening to the heavy silence. His parents had gone to bed hours before.

The house lay in a deep darkness. Brandt couldn't see if the moon shone in the sky or if a street lamp lit up the road outside. No light penetrated the thick veil of trees surrounding the house.

No cars passed by. No wind stirred the leaves on the trees. Brandt listened for the sounds of night birds and insects in the yard. But all was quiet.

Then a faint scratching sound broke the silence.

Brandt froze, listening.

THE SECOND HORROR

Scratch. Scratch. Scratch.

What is that? Brandt wondered, raising his head from the pillow to hear better.

Scratch, scratch, scratch.

Rats, he decided.

In my room.

Chapter 3

 B randt sat straight up in bed and pulled the covers around him for protection.

The scratches grew louder. Brandt listened hard. *Scratch. Scratch-scratch.*

He stared up at the ceiling. The sounds seemed to come from up there.

There is an attic, he remembered. He hadn't seen it yet. But he remembered passing the narrow stairs that led up to it. The sounds grew heavier.

Footsteps, Brandt thought. He turned and lowered his feet to the floor.

Is someone walking around in the attic?

Has someone broken into the house?

Brandt stood up and tiptoed to the door. He peered down the dark hallway. No light came from his parents' bedroom. He knew they must be asleep.

He groped along the hall until he found the door leading to the attic steps. Silently he pulled it open.

He listened.

Silence.

Should he go up?

"Anyone up there?" he called, leaning into the stairwell. His voice came out a hushed whisper. "Who's up there?"

Silence.

Then the soft creaking of the attic floorboards.

Footsteps.

"Who *is* it?"

Silence again.

Brandt took a deep breath and started up the narrow stairs. They felt warm under his bare feet.

He reached the top and peered into the darkness. "Anyone up here?"

His parents were always scolding him for taking matters into his own hands. For being too impulsive.

Reckless, they called it.

Brandt didn't care. He didn't want to think of himself as a wimp.

If someone was in the attic, he wouldn't hide in his bed. He'd go upstairs to check it out.

But the attic was too dark to see anything.

Brandt fumbled along the wall for a light switch.

Then he heard the floorboards creak.

Scratch. Scratch-scratch.

In the darkness, something growled.

Brandt froze.

He heard the click of claws on the floor.

It's coming for me, he realized too late to move out of its way.

With a snarl, the creature sprang through the darkness—its outstretched claws reaching for Brandt's throat.

Chapter 4

"**N**ooooo!"

Brandt let out a terrified wail.

He shielded his head with both arms.

The creature thudded against him, then fell heavily to the floor.

Brandt crouched and waited.

Where was the creature?

Preparing to attack again?

He couldn't see it in the heavy blackness.

But he heard scuttling in the far corner.

I need to see it, Brandt thought frantically. I can't fight it if I can't see it.

He fumbled for the light switch. He found it quickly.

A dim ceiling light clicked on.

Brandt blinked. His eyes moved warily around the room.

The long, narrow attic had a low ceiling over plain plasterboard walls. The dusty floor was littered with boxes. To the right of the door, under the eaves of the house, Brandt spotted a small window, slightly open.

But the creature? No sign of the creature.

Scratch-scratch.

Slowly, carefully, Brandt reached for a straw broom he spotted on top of a box.

The creature stepped out from behind a box.

Brandt narrowed his eyes at it.

A fat raccoon.

He uttered a relieved sigh. Only a raccoon.

But it attacked me, he realized. A raccoon wouldn't do that—unless something was wrong with it.

Unless it had rabies.

He stared at the raccoon. It was breathing hard. Its tail switched back and forth. Through the black mask on its face, it stared back at Brandt—and snarled.

Oh, no, Brandt thought. It *is* rabid.

The raccoon reared back on its haunches, preparing to spring again.

Brandt gripped the broom with both hands. If only I had one of Dad's spears now! he thought.

The raccoon sprang.

With a gasp, Brandt batted at the animal with the broom.

The creature let out an angry hiss as the broom knocked it back to the floor.

Brandt swung at it again. With a furious hiss, the raccoon swiped at the broom with its claws.

Brandt swung the broom. And again furiously. Backing the creature to the wall.

Snarling angrily, the raccoon scrambled up onto the windowsill. It pulled back its lips and bared its pointy teeth at Brandt.

Brandt jabbed at the creature with the broom. The raccoon snatched at the broom with its teeth—and caught it.

Startled, Brandt let the broom slip from his hands. It clattered to the floor.

Brandt started to reach for the broom—but stopped when he noticed the raccoon crouched low, preparing to jump onto him.

If he bent to get the broom, Brandt realized, the raccoon could leap and sink its teeth into his neck.

The raccoon continued to utter its shrill, angry hiss. Spittle dripped from its mouth.

Brandt slowly backed away, his eyes locked on the animal.

His left leg hit something—a chair. With a startled cry, he stumbled and fell backward.

The raccoon sprang again.

Brandt jerked himself up. He grabbed the chair by the legs, lifted it, and jabbed it at the spitting animal.

The raccoon retreated to the windowsill again.

With a loud, angry shout, Brandt heaved the chair at it.

The chair slammed against the wall.

The creature dived out the window.

Brandt lunged for the window, grabbed it by the top of the frame, slid it shut, and locked it.

Struggling to catch his breath, Brandt gazed

blankly around the attic. His entire body trembled. The narrow room appeared to tilt and sway.

A close one, he thought.

That creature put up a real fight.

Had any other animals climbed in through the open attic window? Were there other animals hiding up here?

Brandt wouldn't be able to sleep unless he knew the answer.

Still breathing hard, he made a careful search of the boxes.

No. No more raccoons. No more animals.

I'll be safe now, Brandt thought.

He turned out the light and, his legs weak and rubbery, started downstairs.

His father stood in the hallway in his bathrobe. Brandt stepped into the pale glow from the hall light.

"Brandt? What's going on?" his father asked.

Brandt rubbed the little scar on his cheek. His mother came running out of the bedroom, her features tight with concern.

"Brandt, you look terrible!" she cried. "What happened?"

"I heard noises. In the attic," Brandt replied breathlessly. "I went up to investigate. I—I found a raccoon."

"Is it still up there?" his father demanded, gazing past Brandt to the attic door.

"It's gone," Brandt told them. "I forced it back outside."

"Thank goodness!" Mrs. McCloy cried, raising

both hands to her cheeks. "Who left the attic window open?"

"I—I should tell you something else," Brandt started hesitantly. "I think the raccoon might have had rabies. It was acting very strangely. It attacked me."

Mr. McCloy took Brandt by the arm and began to check him over. "Did it bite you or scratch you anywhere?"

"I don't think so," Brandt said. "I think I'm okay."

"Let's make sure," Mr. McCloy said. He led Brandt into his room and made him stand under the light. Brandt's parents carefully checked his arms, his throat and face, his chest.

"I don't see any marks," Mr. McCloy announced with a sigh of relief.

"But you've got to be more careful, Brandt," his mother said. "What did you think you were doing? You shouldn't have been up there by yourself, trying to fight a rabid raccoon!"

"Your condition, Brandt," his father reminded him.

How could I forget? Brandt thought bitterly. But he kept the thought to himself.

Cally's ghost watched Brandt make his way back to his bedroom. Invisible, she floated in the doorway as he slid into bed, pulling the covers up to his chin.

Nice going, Brandt, Cally thought, a scornful smile playing over her lips.

I wish I could tell you how much I enjoyed your big scene in the attic just now.

But I'm not quite ready to reveal myself to you. I will, though. Soon, I will.

You are turning out to be very entertaining, Brandt. I enjoyed watching you fight that raccoon.

I haven't had so much fun in ages.

You're so cute looking when you're scared, Brandt. I like the way your big brown eyes flash, and the way your jaw sticks out when you clench your teeth.

Cute. Real cute.

Cally watched Brandt roll onto his side.

Can't get to sleep, huh? she thought. Still thinking about your narrow escape?

Well, you don't have to worry about getting rabies, Brandt. That raccoon didn't have rabies.

There's another reason that it acted so strangely. There's something else that made it act viciously.

The evil, Brandt. The evil in this house.

But there will be time to discover that. Plenty of time.

Better get your sleep, Brandt. Better rest up, Cally told him silently.

Because I have lots of excitement in store for you.

You and I are going to be really good friends.

Chapter 5

Brandt slept late the next morning. His room was dark, but glancing at his clock, he saw that it was already after ten. Through the thick cover of trees outside the window, he thought he spotted a patch of blue October sky.

A sunny Sunday, he thought with satisfaction. A good day for a long drive. I've got to get away from Mom and Dad for a couple of hours. They're working my nerves.

Downstairs he found his parents in the driveway unloading groceries from the battered blue minivan.

"Go help your mother," his father ordered. "There's a twelve-pound turkey in the backseat, and I don't want her to strain her back lifting it."

Brandt carried the turkey into the house for his

mother. "We practically bought out the store," she told him. "I've got roast beef, chicken, vegetables, cake mix— What would you like for dinner tonight, Brandt?"

"Roast beef sounds good," Brandt replied, shoving the turkey into the refrigerator.

"I'll make a devil's food cake too," Mrs. McCloy said.

"Have you finished unpacking your room, Brandt?" his father asked.

"I haven't even started," Brandt admitted. "I'll get to it. But I thought I'd go for a drive first, check out the area. Can I take the Honda?"

His father frowned. "We've got a lot of settling in to do. I was hoping you'd finish in your room and start unpacking the books."

"I'll get to it," Brandt promised, picking up the car keys from the kitchen table and jiggling them in one hand. "I won't be gone long."

"Brandt!" his father protested.

Brandt dashed out the back door before they could stop him. He jumped into the dark green Honda and quickly backed around the van and down the driveway.

His parents ran to the front yard, waving their arms at him, motioning for him to come back. He pretended not to see them. Lowering his foot hard on the gas pedal, he roared off down Fear Street.

He sped up even more when his house vanished from sight. The old houses whirred by. Slender beams of morning sunshine poked through the old trees that lined the street. He rolled down the window and let the cool autumn air wash over his face.

This is just what I needed, he told himself. To get out of the house, to get moving, to feel the air.

With a squeal of tires, he turned off Fear Street and headed out of town. He jammed a cassette into the tape deck and cranked up the volume.

He sang along with the music. " 'Don't care if I live, don't care if I die.' "

Nothing but farm fields on both sides now. A long, twisting highway, nearly empty.

Okay, let's see how fast I can go! he thought.

He jammed his foot down and watched the speedometer climb. Seventy miles an hour. Eighty. He flew around the tight curves, spinning the wheel, enjoying the excitement of not knowing what lay around the next curve.

The road climbed into low brown hills. Brandt blasted the music and kept his foot jammed down on the accelerator. The road veered to the right and then sharply left.

He gazed out over a deep gorge that plunged straight down to his right. A narrow river wound through the valley far below, sparkling in the sun.

Beautiful, he thought, following the course of the river with his eyes.

When he turned back to the road, the red oil truck already filled the windshield.

I'm in the left lane! Brandt realized in panic.

He cried out and frantically cut the wheel back to the right.

But the car bounced out of control.

Too far! Too far to the right!

The oil truck's airhorn rose like a siren.

He slammed his foot down on the brake.

The car skidded across the wide shoulder—heading straight toward the deep gorge.

Chapter 6

Gripping the wheel with both hands, his foot all the way down on the brake, Brandt shut his eyes.

And waited for the fall.

Waited for the long slide down.

When the car didn't move, he opened his eyes—and saw that the car wasn't moving.

"Oh, man!" he cried, jumping out of the car. The right front tire hung over the edge of the gorge. The other three were safely on solid ground.

"Oh, man," he repeated, shaking his head.

He hurried back into the small Honda. Brandt shifted into reverse and pressed the gas pedal. The tires skidded in the dirt. The car slipped, but in the wrong direction—farther out over the gorge.

"Come on!" Brandt shouted to the car.

When he hit the gas this time the rear tires caught the road and pulled the car back. The right front wheel eased up over the edge of the gorge and back onto the shoulder.

Brandt stopped for a second and caught his breath. Then he made a U-turn and sped back toward home at eighty miles an hour.

"That was fun," he said out loud. "Man, that was fun!"

That night Brandt lay restlessly in the darkness, waiting for sleep.

I'm so tired from putting up bookshelves and unpacking boxes all afternoon, he thought. So why can't I get to sleep?

He stared at the ceiling. He listened for raccoon scratches.

Silence.

So why did he have this strange feeling, the feeling that something was hovering nearby. Something dangerous.

It must be moving into an unfamiliar house, he told himself. Or maybe it's the thought that tomorrow is my first day in a new high school.

Shadyside High.

And I'll be the new kid. The kid who doesn't know anyone.

He glanced at the clock. I've *got* to get some sleep, he thought. Or else tomorrow I'll have dark circles around my eyes like that raccoon.

He felt himself drifting off.

He closed his eyes.

A soft whisper of cold air rippled across his skin.

He opened his eyes.

Where did it come from?

Another puff of cold air. Like an icy breath.

Is someone here? he thought. His skin tingled.

He felt the brush of lips on the back of his neck. Cold, cold lips.

And then sharp teeth bit into his shoulder—and he screamed.

Chapter 7

The overhead light clicked on. Mr. Mc-Cloy rushed to Brandt's side. "What's wrong? What happened?" He grabbed Brandt's trembling shoulders and tried to calm him.

Brandt swallowed hard. "My—my neck—" he managed to choke out. He rubbed the spot with his hand. It still felt cold.

"You hurt your neck? You have a stiff neck?" Brandt's father demanded, his voice clogged with sleep. "Let me see it."

Brandt leaned forward. "Something—bit my neck," he said. "Can you see where?"

"I don't see anything," Mr. McCloy replied, lowering his head and squinting at the back of Brandt's neck.

"Another r-raccoon?" Brandt stammered.

"I hope not," his father muttered. He searched

the room with his eyes. Then he bent down and checked under the bed. He pulled open the closet door and riffled through Brandt's clothes. He checked under the desk, inside boxes—all over the room.

Mr. McCloy let out a weary, relieved sigh. "Must have been a dream, Brandt. A nightmare."

Brandt rubbed the back of his neck. It felt okay now. His hand moved to the scar on his cheek. "It was so real, Dad. I really thought—"

"You're nervous about school tomorrow. That's all," Mr. McCloy assured him. "Try to get some sleep, okay?"

"Okay."

Mr. McCloy switched off the light as he left the room. Brandt settled down in the darkness. He pulled the covers up to his chin. "A dream," he muttered softly. "Just a stupid dream."

He had almost drifted off to sleep, when he felt a cold rush of air on his face again.

Brandt heard the roar of a vacuum cleaner as he started downstairs the next morning. Peeking into the living room, he was startled to see a short, squat, gray-haired woman vacuuming. Brandt had never seen her before.

"Hi," he called, but the woman didn't glance up. Brandt figured she couldn't hear him over the roar. He went into the kitchen.

"Good morning, Brandt," his father greeted him from the table. "Did you manage to get some sleep last night?"

"A little," Brandt replied. "Who's that woman in the living room?"

"Her name is Mrs. Nordstrom," Mrs. McCloy told him. "She's going to help me unpack and get the house into shape. Did you meet her? She's very nice."

"I tried to say hello, but she had the vacuum cleaner going," Brandt explained. "Where did she come from?"

"Mr. Hankers recommended her the other day," Mrs. McCloy said. "I was going to phone her this morning to see if she wanted a job. But she showed up before I even got a chance to call. I guess Mr. Hankers called her for me."

"She used to work for the previous owners of the house," Mr. McCloy added.

"Do you want juice this morning, Brandt?" his mother asked. She opened a carton on the counter and pulled out a couple of juice glasses. "Just a little? Since it's your first day at your new school?"

"No, thanks," Brandt said. He never ate breakfast, and his mother knew it. But she couldn't stop pestering him about it anyway.

He sat down at the table while his father read the newspaper and drank his coffee. His mother began to store the juice glasses in a cabinet.

"I keep thinking about last night," Brandt said. "That—that bite on my neck . . ."

Raising his head from the newspaper, Mr. McCloy glanced across the room to his wife. She turned from the cabinet and met her husband's gaze with a worried expression.

"I don't think it was a nightmare," Brandt continued thoughtfully. "It seemed too real."

"Brandt—" His mother sat down at the table, absentmindedly gripping two glasses in her hands.

"Do you really think there was someone in your room last night?" Mr. McCloy demanded, his eyes locked on Brandt. "I checked everywhere. Even under the bed."

"No—not a person," Brandt replied, running a hand back through his dark, wavy hair. "But something. A spirit of some kind." He smiled. "Maybe the house is haunted."

Brandt's father chuckled. He set down his newspaper. "Maybe my research is rubbing off on you—playing on your imagination. After all, you've grown up in all kinds of strange places, hearing me talk about magic and spirits—"

"Maybe," Brandt admitted. "But I don't think so."

Mr. McCloy rubbed his hands together and smiled. "Hmmm. It's kind of tempting. Exciting. What if there *is* some kind of spirit right here in our own house?"

Brandt's mother flashed him a disgusted look. "Can't we be serious? There aren't ghosts and spirits floating around *everywhere* in the world, you know? I'm sure the house is perfectly safe," she insisted.

"Maybe it's haunted, and maybe it's not," Mr. McCloy said firmly. "There could be other explanations."

"But you'll check it out?" Brandt asked.

"Of course. How could I resist?"

"Thanks, Dad."

Brandt's mother glanced at the kitchen clock. "You'd better get going, Brandt," she said.

Brandt stood up. "I wanted to get there a little early. I was thinking I might try to meet a few kids before my first class."

"Just don't overdo it, Brandt," his father warned. "Remember—"

"I know, I know. I'll be careful," Brandt groaned.

He grabbed his backpack from the hall table and started out the door.

The day was bright and warm for October, but the McCloys' front yard lay in dark shadow. The trees and bushes were so thick they nearly blocked out the sunlight. Some of the leaves on the trees had turned yellow and red, but they clung to their branches as if for dear life.

Brandt pulled the collar of his jeans jacket close around his neck. He started across the front yard, through the thicket of bushes and trees.

This grass is so tall, he thought, kicking a path through the high blades. Mowing it is going to be a nightmare. Maybe that guy Hankers will do it.

As he moved toward the sidewalk, he gazed at the sunlight that fell onto the street. As soon as my front yard ends, the sunlight begins, he thought.

Weird.

He was stepping onto the sidewalk, when something pushed him, hard, from behind. An icy hand tightened itself on his shoulder.

Chapter 8

With a startled gasp, Brandt spun around. And stared into the face of a girl about his age.

"I'm sorry. I tripped," she explained, blushing. "I didn't mean to grab you."

She was small and pretty, blond, with bright blue eyes. She wore a short gray plaid wool skirt over black tights, and an oversize pale blue sweater.

Brandt relaxed. "You scared me," he confessed. "Do you live around here?"

She nodded. "I'm Abbie Ayler," she told him, straightening her sweater. "I'm not usually such a total klutz. How's the new house? I saw you moving in the other day."

"It's okay," Brandt replied. "A little run-down though." He told her his name. "Are you heading for school?"

"Yeah, but I'm not going your way," Abbie replied. "You're going to Shadyside High, right?"

Brandt nodded. "You don't go there?"

"No. Darwin Academy." She made a face. "It's a girls school."

"Oh," Brandt said. "Too bad."

Abbie laughed. "Tell me about it." She tossed back her blond hair. "So, it's hard to move, huh? Makes you a little nervous? Or do you always jump three feet in the air when someone grabs your shoulder?"

"I'm a little stressed," Brandt admitted with a shrug.

"It's dark in your yard, isn't it?" Abbie said, her blue eyes catching the sunlight. "All those big old trees."

"Yeah. Pretty dark."

"I suppose you've heard the stories about the house," she said quietly.

"Stories? What kind of stories?" Brandt demanded.

Abbie shrugged. "I don't know. Stories about the people who used to live here. I think something bad happened to them."

"Huh? What happened?"

"I'm not really sure," Abbie replied, staring up at the house. "People tell different stories. You know how it is."

"Did you know the family who lived here before?" Brandt asked, switching his backpack to his other shoulder.

"Not really," Abbie told him. "I saw the two girls

once, I think. They were twins, but they didn't look exactly alike. Anyway, they didn't stay long."

"Why not?" Brandt asked.

Abbie hesitated. "I heard one of the girls died."

"That's awful," Brandt exclaimed. "You mean she died right in my house?"

Abbie nodded. "Yeah. I guess. Pretty horrible, huh?" She didn't give him time to reply. "My uncle—he says there's some kind of curse on the house. Like it's evil or something."

Evil?

Brandt felt a cold chill. He thought of the raccoon that attacked him. And he thought of the cold lips on the back of his neck, the teeth that dug into his skin.

"But I'm sure that's just a lot of silly gossip," Abbie added, seeing the troubled expression on Brandt's face. "I mean, people tell all kinds of weird stories about Fear Street." She let out an awkward laugh.

"You'll have to tell me some of the stories sometime," Brandt told her. *She's really great looking,* he thought. *I think I'm going to like having her for a neighbor!*

But her words continued to trouble him. He glanced up at the house, resting in the shadows of the huge, dark trees.

Then something caught his eye.

Something moved in an upstairs window. Something dark. It swung heavily behind the glass.

Brandt stared harder.

The dark shape swayed in the window of his parents' room. Brandt blinked and stared again, afraid to believe his own eyes.

It couldn't be true.

But it was.

His father's body was hanging in the window.

Chapter 9

Brandt heard Abbie scream.

He turned to see her pointing up at the window. She saw it too.

Without saying a word, Brandt ran blindly through the tall grass, up onto the porch, into the house. Abbie followed close behind.

"Dad!" Brandt screamed frantically as he flew up the stairs. "Dad!"

He stumbled and fell against the wall, then burst into his parents' room.

"Dad!"

"Brandt? What on earth is the matter?" Mrs. McCloy stood calmly by the bed, plumping up a pillow. "What's wrong, Brandt?"

"Huh?" Brandt uttered a choked cry.

The bathroom door opened. Brandt gaped in shock as his father stepped out.

"What's going on?" Mr. McCloy demanded sharply. "I saw you leave for school."

Brandt turned to the window. One of his father's suits was hanging there.

"Oh, wow," Brandt muttered.

He heard giggling behind him. Abbie stepped up beside him, her eyes on the suit.

Brandt burst out laughing too. "A suit!" he cried. "It's only a suit!"

"Brandt—have you totally lost it?" his mother demanded. His parents stared at him as if he had gone completely mad.

"I'm sorry," Brandt said, finally pulling himself together. "We thought you were that suit, Dad."

Mr. McCloy frowned and shook his head. "I don't get it."

"This is Abbie," Brandt told his parents. "She's a neighbor."

"It's nice to meet you, Abbie," Mrs. McCloy said. "But, Brandt, I wish you wouldn't bring guests into our bedroom like this. I haven't even made the bed yet."

"I'm sorry, Mom," Brandt said. "It was a mistake. A major mistake." He and Abbie exchanged amused glances.

"We'd better get going," Abbie said, starting out of the room. "It was nice to meet you."

Brandt and Abbie ran downstairs and outside the house, laughing all the way.

"I really thought it was a man hanging in the window," Abbie exclaimed. "Your parents must think I'm crazy! Or else very rude."

"I could've sworn it was my dad," Brandt admitted. "I—I was so scared." He smiled at her. He wondered if she liked him. Or did she just think he was weird?

"Would you like to get together on Saturday afternoon?" he asked her. "Maybe we could study together or something."

"Yeah. Great," Abbie replied, smiling back at him. "I'll come over around two, okay?"

"Okay!" Brandt glanced at his watch. "Oh, man. I'm off to a great start. Late for my first day of school!"

He waved to her and hurried down Fear Street to catch the bus to Shadyside High.

Brandt stood in line at the cafeteria, tray in hand. The odor of brussels sprouts floated out of the kitchen. The girl ahead of him in line wrinkled her nose and said sarcastically, "Smells great, huh? I'll bet you never had food like this at your old school."

"At my old school we had steak every day," Brandt joked. "We begged for salad and green beans and brussels sprouts. But they gave us French fries instead."

The girl smiled. She was tall and pretty, with straight black hair to her shoulders and dramatic blue eyes under heavy black eyebrows. She wore faded jeans, torn at both knees, and a cropped white sweater.

"I heard there was a new kid," she said, examining Brandt with her dramatic eyes. "You're him, huh?"

Brandt grinned. "Yeah. I'm all new. The new, improved me. I moved here on Saturday." He introduced himself.

"Welcome to Shadyside, Brandt," the girl said. "I'm Jinny Thompson." The line began to move, and Jinny added, "You'd better let me take you on a guided tour of the steam trays. I'd hate for you to get sick on your first day at school."

Brandt picked out a knife and a fork and set them on his tray. A girl with short auburn hair squeezed between him and Jinny. "Let me cut in, Jinny," she insisted. "The line's really long, and I'm starving. I had half a Snickers bar for breakfast. That's all. Really."

The red-haired girl stood a couple of inches shorter than Jinny. She had a bulky black sweater pulled down almost to her knees over bright green leggings.

She's really cute too, Brandt thought. He reached behind him, pulled a tray from the stack, and handed it to Jinny's friend.

"Thanks." She flashed him a toothy smile. "You must be the new kid."

"His name is Brandt Something-or-Other, and he's very nice," Jinny told her. "But I'm sure it will wear off after a while. It always does." She grinned at Brandt to let him know she was teasing. "This is my friend Meg. Meg Morris."

"What's up with the trays? Why are they always wet?" Meg demanded, staring in disgust at the plastic lunch tray. "Lunch hasn't even started, and the trays are all wet. Why is that?"

"It's a special kind of plastic," Brandt joked. "It stays wet no matter what you do to it."

Both girls laughed. Meg had a funny, high-pitched laugh that sounded more like whistling than laughing.

The line began to move. Jinny opened a refrigerator case and took out a salad wrapped in cellophane.

"Check out this lettuce," she said, showing the salad to Brandt. "It must have turned brown, so they bleached it white."

"So why are you eating it?" he asked.

"Wait till you see what the other choices are," Meg said, rolling her eyes.

Jinny and Meg told Brandt more than he wanted to know about the food in the cafeteria. He managed to get through the line with a ham and cheese sandwich and a carton of milk.

He followed Meg and Jinny to a table in the back of the room. A tall, blond, athletic-looking boy ambled over, a basketball tucked under one arm. He sat next to Jinny and draped his other arm casually around the shoulders of her white sweater.

"Hey, Jin," he said. "Hey, Meg." He narrowed his eyes at Brandt and nodded to him.

"Jon Burks, this is Brandt McCloy," Jinny announced. "He's new. Be nice to him."

"Why wouldn't I be nice to him?" Jon replied, pretending to be insulted. "I'm a nice guy. Ask anybody." He spun the basketball on his finger. "You play ball?" he asked Brandt.

"Not really," Brandt replied.

"You ought to try out for the team," Jon suggested. "We need tall guys."

Mom would go totally ballistic if I told her I wanted to play basketball, Brandt thought. She's always nagging me to be careful.

But he found himself thinking: I wonder if I could make the team?

I'm good at sports. I never played in a league or anything. Just fooled around on the playground with my friends. It might be fun to play on a team. And I'd get to meet a lot of guys.

I'll go to a few practices, he decided. It can't hurt. Then maybe I'll try out. Mom and Dad never have to know.

"Hey, Brandt." Jon snapped his fingers, interrupting Brandt's thoughts. "You still with us?"

"What time is practice?" Brandt asked.

"You're going to try out? That's excellent!" Meg exclaimed.

Jinny rolled her eyes. "Don't let Jon push you around, Brandt."

"We have practice every afternoon at three-thirty," Jon told Brandt, ignoring Jinny. "And tryouts are next week."

He turned to Jinny and asked, "You're meeting me after practice—right?"

Jinny shook her head. "No way. With all that French homework and the term paper to get started?"

"You're worried about homework?" Jon shook his head in disbelief. "That's a new one." He

glanced suspiciously at Brandt. Then he stood up abruptly.

"I hope you get all your homework done before Friday," he said. "Don't forget—we're going out Friday night. I had to really fight to get the car."

"I won't forget," Jinny promised. "No problem."

Jon left without saying good bye, dribbling his basketball across the cafeteria floor.

"What's with him?" Meg asked.

Jinny shrugged. "Who knows? That's how Jon is. He gets jealous if I sit alone and read a book."

She flashed Brandt a teasing smile and added, "But I never let that stop me from doing what I want."

"Hey—you made it, McCloy." Jon shoved a basketball into Brandt's arms as Brandt entered the gym that afternoon. "Hey, guys!" He called to five or six other boys, who were warming up across the floor. "This is him! The new guy! He says he's the next superstar! He says his nickname is In Your Face!"

"No way! No, I didn't!" Brandt cried, feeling his face go red.

"You told me you were all-state last year!" Jon claimed loudly enough so that everyone in the gym could hear it.

"Give me a break!" Brandt protested. Why was Jon doing this to him? Was he just goofing? Or did he really want to embarrass Brandt?

Jon took a ball, dribbled to the far end of the gym, and started practicing foul shots. Brandt slowly and easily dribbled the ball down the court. He spun around and dribbled back the other way, warming up.

This is going to be a breeze, he thought. Nothing to worry about.

A tall, fortyish-looking bald man wearing gray sweats stopped Brandt on the sideline. "I'm Coach Hurley," he announced, fiddling with the whistle that hung from his neck. "You're the new kid, right? What year are you?"

"Eleventh grade," Brandt replied.

"Good. Did you play at your old school?"

Brandt nearly smiled at the thought of playing basketball on the island of Mapolo. "No," he replied. "But I think I can be good at it."

Mr. Hurley checked him out. "Well, you're certainly tall enough. If you're tall and you're breathing, you've got a pretty good chance of making this team," he said dryly. "We'll start scrimmaging in a few minutes. We'll see what you can do."

Later, Jon threw a blue jersey over his head and tossed Brandt a red one. They stood on opposite sides of the court, on different teams.

Coach Hurley blew his whistle. The centers jumped for the ball. It bounced to Jon.

Jon dribbled down the court and took a shot. Brandt tried to block him. Brandt timed his jump carefully—and slapped Jon's ball away from the basket.

"Good, McCloy!" Coach Hurley shouted.

Jon grunted.

Brandt ran down the court with his teammates.

A short, wiry boy with curly black hair passed the ball to him. Brandt took a shot. Missed.

The blue team had the ball again. Brandt ran back down the court, guarding Jon.

Brandt panted, trying to catch his breath. A line of sweat trickled down his forehead. He glanced at the other guys to see how much they were sweating. Most of them weren't.

No problem, Brandt told himself. I'm just a little out of shape, that's all.

Jon slipped past Brandt and went up for a lay-up. The ball *swoosh*ed in.

Back down the court. Brandt lagged behind his teammates. His arms and legs felt as if they weighed a thousand pounds.

Breathing hard, he stopped running and bent over, resting his hands on his knees.

"You can't be tired already, McCloy!" he heard Coach Hurley calling. "Make sure you do an extra five laps after practice."

Brandt nodded, breathless.

I can do it, he told himself. I can. I can.

I will.

I need a good alibi, an excuse, Brandt thought as he ambled down Fear Street toward home that evening. Mom will never get off my case if she finds out I've been playing basketball.

The sun had already lowered itself behind the old trees. A cool, gusting wind carried a hint of winter.

As he stared up at his new house, 99 Fear Street, Brandt suddenly remembered Abbie's words that morning. A girl died in my house, he thought, shuddering.

The house is evil, Abbie had said.

The whole street is evil.

He gazed around at the neighbors' houses. They all seemed as old and dark as his. Which one does Abbie live in? he wondered.

He took a deep breath, trying to think of an excuse for being late, and hurried inside.

He found his mother talking to Mr. Hankers. "I hope you're right," she was saying. "I can't stand to think of living with rats in the basement."

"I don't think they'll bother you anymore," Mr. Hankers replied, scratching his black hair. "If they do, just let me know." He smiled at Brandt on his way out.

"Where have you been, Brandt?" Mrs. McCloy asked. "It's dark out already."

"Well—" Brandt hesitated. "The student senate. I decided to join. I thought I'd meet some kids there."

His mother smiled. "That sounds perfect for you," she said.

"It meets every day after school," Brandt told her. "I've already got tons of homework. I'd better go upstairs and get started."

She wanted to hear more about his first day. But he hurried up to his room and shut the door. He didn't want her to see how tired he was.

Without bothering to turn on the light, he dropped onto his bed. He sniffed.

"Hey." Something smells weird in here, he thought.

He sat up.

That smell again. So sour. Getting stronger.

"Wow." It—it's awful, Brandt thought as the stench rose around him. It smells like—

He didn't want to think about what it smelled like. But he knew.

It smelled like decay. Like rotten meat.

I'm going to be sick, he thought.

He jumped up and started to the window to let in some fresh air.

But he stopped when he saw a light under his closet door.

There *is* no light in my closet, Brandt remembered.

He took a step closer, his eyes on the floor. The light was green, a sickening green glow that seemed to grow brighter as Brandt stared at it.

He took another step toward the closet. Then another.

What could be inside?

He put his hand on the doorknob—and immediately jerked it back.

The doorknob felt wet and slimy.

Brandt stared at his hand. It was covered in a disgusting green goo. He rubbed it on his jeans.

The slime stuck to his hand.

The green glow brightened, casting the entire room in its sickening green.

The foul odor rose up around him.

I've got to get out of here, he thought.

But no. He had to find out what was inside the closet.

What was behind that door?

He swallowed his nausea and forced himself back to the closet door.

He gripped the slimy doorknob and turned it.

The closet door pulled open.

A flash of white light.

What was it?

What was in there?

He didn't see it until it was too late.

And then it sprang out at him, choking off his terrified scream.

Chapter 10

A flash of white. Heavy like smoke. Choking and sour.

It burst from the closet as if shot out, and covered Brandt's face in a white cloud.

It—it's *strangling* me, Brandt realized.

He tore at the cloud wildly, frantically. But he couldn't grab hold of it.

Coughing, sputtering, and gasping for air, he staggered blindly toward the door to his room. And fell to his knees.

The door swung open. The light came on. Mrs. McCloy uttered a frightened cry. "Brandt—what are you doing down there?"

"Huh?" He gazed up at her, struggling to focus his eyes. "Mom?"

She dropped down beside him. "Brandt?"

"Mom, I—uh—" Brandt stared at the open closet door.

What had happened? It was all gone now.

No choking white cloud. No green glow.

No putrid stench of death.

All vanished the instant his mother opened the door.

But Brandt knew it would be back.

It's after me, Brandt thought, unable to stop the trembling that convulsed his entire body.

Something is in this house—and it's after me.

Well, well. You're beginning to get it now, Brandt, Cally's ghost thought.

She laughed, watching him pace nervously back and forth in his room. He examined the closet for the tenth time. Then he sat down on the bed and stared at the ceiling, thinking hard.

You're a smart boy, Brandt, Cally thought scornfully.

You're beginning to understand.

Something *is* after you.

I'm after you.

Coach Hurley blew his whistle. "One on one!" he shouted. "Line up."

It was the next afternoon. Brandt stood at half-court, the basketball in his hand.

Turning to one side, he saw Jinny and Meg watching from the bleachers. Jinny waved to him and shouted something he couldn't hear.

Hope I don't mess up, Brandt thought. He'd been

thinking a lot about both girls. He didn't want to embarrass himself in front of them.

"Burks, McCloy—go ahead!" Coach Hurley ordered.

Why does the coach always pair me up with Jon? Brandt wondered miserably. He must think we're friends or something.

"Come on, McCloy. Let's go," Jon taunted.

Brandt bounced the basketball. He crouched low, trying to dribble past Jon and shoot a basket. Jon guarded him closely.

"Watch for fouls, Burks!" the coach yelled at Jon. "You led the team in fouls last year. I'm keeping my eye on you."

Brandt charged hard, trying to slip past Jon. Finally, with a loud groan of effort, he dodged to the left and took his shot.

The ball hit the rim and dropped in.

Scowling, Jon snatched the ball and ran to half-court. Brandt set his legs, prepared to guard him.

Jon dribbled toward the basket. Brandt backed up, trying to stay with him.

Then, with a burst of speed, Jon charged right into him.

"Hey!" Brandt cried out as he toppled over backward. He landed hard on one elbow. Pain shot up his arm as the elbow scraped over the hardwood floor.

The coach blew his whistle. "Jon! I warned you!"

"I didn't touch him!" Jon protested. "He tripped!"

Shaken, Brandt sat up quickly to examine his

elbow. He gasped as he saw the black bruise spread across his arm like a dark stain.

No! he thought, frozen in horror, watching the black stain widen.

My condition . . .

The stain darkened and spread up his arm.

How can I keep everyone from seeing it? Brandt wondered.

Too late, he realized, gazing up.

Coach Hurley and all the players were staring down at him in horror.

Chapter 11

Brandt covered part of the blackening bruise with his other hand. Coach Hurley leaned over him, his eyes narrowed with concern. "You okay?" he demanded, staring at Brandt's arm. "That's a nasty-looking bruise. I didn't think you fell that hard."

"No big deal," Brandt replied, trying to sound calm. He turned, moving the arm out of view. "It doesn't hurt."

"Sit out the rest of the practice anyway, just in case," Coach Hurley advised.

"Really, I'm all right," Brandt insisted.

The coach shrugged. "Whatever you say."

Brandt trotted unsteadily back to the others. He saw Jon dribbling the ball casually at the foul line.

As Brandt moved past, he caught the triumphant grin on Jon's face.

Brandt lay awake that night as the faces of the kids he'd met floated through his mind. He pictured Abbie, her lively blue eyes, her straight blond hair, her musical laugh.

Jinny and Meg entered his thoughts. They both flirted with him whenever they saw him. It was obvious they were competing for him—even though Jinny was already going with Jon.

Jon . . .

Have I already made an enemy? Brandt wondered.

Jon . . .

Bad practice today, Brandt thought, rubbing his elbow. The bruise had already started to fade. But Coach Hurley had stared at it, stared at Brandt suspiciously.

Tomorrow will be better, Brandt vowed. I'll show Hurley how tough I am.

Creak.

The faces disappeared from Brandt's mind as he heard the sound above his head.

A footstep. Then another.

Brandt sat up in bed, listening.

Creak, creak.

Footsteps. Someone was walking around in the attic.

Don't go up there, Brandt told himself. Just stay here. Stay here and be safe.

But he knew he couldn't do that.

Creak, creak, creak.

He climbed out of bed and tiptoed into the dark hallway. His parents were asleep. Their door was closed.

The door to the attic opened with a soft squeak. Brandt leaned in and listened for the footsteps.

He heard them. Steady, even steps, as if someone were pacing over the creaking floorboards.

Brandt silently crept up the stairs. He fumbled against the wall. Clicked on the light.

The long, low room was a shimmering blur. He squinted hard, waiting for his eyes to adjust.

No one there.

Weird, Brandt thought. I heard the footsteps just a second ago.

He searched the attic, behind all the boxes and crates. No one.

He spotted something in the middle of the floor. A small notebook.

How could I have missed that? he asked himself, staring hard at it.

It was as if someone had put it there on purpose.

Brandt sat on the floor and opened the notebook.

It was a diary, he quickly discovered. A girl's diary. She'd written her name on the first page.

CALLY FRASIER.

Brandt flipped through the pages. This must be the diary of one of those twins who used to live here, he thought. One of the girls Abbie told me about.

He skipped the parts in the beginning that seemed to be about some boy Cally liked. But then he came to a passage that interested him:

Anthony is so cute. He told us the most unbelievable story today. Of course Kody swallowed every word of it. My poor sister is so gullible. I have to admit it was scary. But it can't be true. How could it?

Anthony said there's a reason why our house seems so creepy. He told us about a man named Simon Fear. Anthony said Simon Fear and his wife, Angelica, were early settlers here. They used to live in a mansion down the street. Our street is named after them.

The Fears were really rich, and really strange. They tortured people and killed them. Angelica was really into weird stuff, Anthony said. And she used real live people to try out her strange powers.

Brandt turned the page and continued reading.

The Fears buried their victims in a secret graveyard. This all took place about a hundred years ago. Then, about thirty years ago, when workers were building this house, they found the graves. But they went ahead and built the house on top of the graveyard.

When the house was finished, the family who built it came to look at it. A man, his wife, and his two kids.

The man left his family in the living room for a few minutes—and when he came back, he found them dead. Anthony swears that their heads were missing. Something or someone had ripped their heads right off their necks! It's so gross!

Brandt set the diary down to take this in. *Something or someone had ripped their heads right off their necks.*

A wave of nausea rose from his stomach. But he picked up the diary and read on.

> *That family never moved in, of course. No one did—until us. Of course Dad would be the first person in thirty years to buy the place!*
>
> *Now Kody is positive the house is haunted. I don't believe in any of that stuff—but I have to admit, there's something weird about this place. And Anthony's story was really scary. . . .*

Brandt shut the diary.

I was right, he thought grimly. This house was built on a cursed spot. It *is* haunted.

I wonder what happened to Cally Frasier, he thought. I wonder where she lives now, what she's doing. I wonder why she left her diary behind.

An unpleasant thought gripped him: Abbie said that one of the sisters had died. Was it Cally?

He set the diary on the floor where he found it. It fell open to the last page.

Brandt glanced at it, and a chill ran through his body as his question was answered.

On the top of the page, in blue ink, Cally had written: *I died tonight.*

* * *

Mr. Ross, Brandt's chemistry teacher, rapped on his desk for attention. "People!" he shouted. The room grew quieter.

Brandt sat in the back row of the classroom. On his left sat Meg. On his right, Jinny, then Jon. Jinny was wearing a black miniskirt, black tights, and a black sweater to match her black hair.

She looks awesome, Brandt thought.

"Now that we've covered a lot of the basics of chemistry," Mr. Ross began, "we're ready to start our lab work. You'll each need a partner. I'll give you ten minutes to sort it out."

The room erupted into loud discussions. Jon said, "We're lab partners, right, Jinny?"

But Jinny gave Brandt a sly glance and replied, "Well, Jon, I don't know. Brandt and I already talked about being lab partners. I sort of promised him. Didn't I, Brandt?"

She turned to Brandt.

Brandt hesitated. He saw Jon scowling at him. This was the first he'd heard any talk about lab partners. But it would be fun to work with Jinny, he thought. And it would be fun to make Jon even more jealous.

"Yeah, right," he told her. "A promise is a promise."

Jinny grinned.

"Jinny, you're sitting next to Jon," Meg complained. "I'll be Brandt's lab partner."

"No way. I promised Brandt," Jinny insisted.

Meg let out an exasperated sigh. "Jinny, what's your problem? We're only talking about lab partners here. You'll be Jon's partner and I'll be Brandt's. It's easier that way."

"Why don't you be Jon's lab partner?" Jinny suggested with a sly grin. "That's just as easy."

"That settles it," Brandt announced. "Meg and Jon are lab partners. Jinny's my partner. I'll go tell Mr. Ross."

The bell rang just as Brandt stood up to go to Mr. Ross's desk. Brandt could feel Jon's eyes burning a hole in the back of his head.

The teacher wrote down the partner assignments, and the students filed noisily out of the classroom.

Brandt found Jinny waiting for him in the hall. "I hope you don't mind my little lie," she said. "I mean, what I said about promising to be your lab partner. I just didn't want to work with Jon. He's so bad at chemistry, and he'd make me do all the work."

"Hey, no problem," Brandt told her. "Listen, why don't you come over to my house this Saturday? We can get a head start on our project."

Jinny's dark eyes lit up. She flashed her dazzling smile at Brandt. "That sounds great. Where do you live?"

"On Fear Street. Ninety-nine Fear Street."

Jinny's smile faded. "Ninety-nine . . . Fear Street? Are you serious?"

Brandt nodded. "Yeah. I'm serious."

"Weird," she murmured.

"It's just a house," Brandt replied with a shrug.

"Well—it can't be all bad if you live there," she said softly, her eyes locked on his.

"Excellent!" Brandt exclaimed. "Come over around two."

He watched her as she walked down the hall to her next class.

Yes! he thought. Excellent.

Now—how to get Mom and Dad out of the house?

"Okay! Lay-ups!" Coach Hurley's deep voice echoed through the gym.

Brandt lined up with the other guys to run down the court, leap into the air, and shoot the ball into the basket with one hand.

When his turn came, Brandt dribbled the ball quickly and smoothly, and went for a graceful lay-up. The ball rolled inside the rim and dropped out.

I'll make the next one, he thought. He knew he'd looked good making the shot, at least.

Jon took his turn after Brandt. His lay-up swished perfectly through the hoop. He glanced at Brandt after the shot went through.

Yeah, I saw it, Jon, Brandt thought, rolling his eyes.

"Great shot, Jon. Let's see you do it again," Brandt shouted.

"Let's see you do it *once!*" Jon taunted.

Brandt's next lay-up was as graceful as the first. His lanky arms and legs moved in perfect symmetry.

And this time the ball dropped through the basket with a *swish*.

He didn't glance at Jon to check his reaction.

Instead, he coolly trotted back to the line as if nothing special had happened.

Jon's next shot barely missed.

Jon stood behind Brandt in line and whispered, "It's a tie. One to one. Best out of three?"

Brandt nodded. He shook his arms and legs. They began to feel heavy and tired.

Come on, he urged himself. Don't give out on me. Just one more shot.

The guy ahead of Brandt passed him the ball. Brandt caught it and dribbled toward the basket.

He leapt for the shot, the ball in his right hand. He stretched his right arm high into the air.

"Owwww!"

He cried out as he heard a loud *snap*.

Chapter 12

A sharp jolt shot through his shoulder.

Screeching in pain, Brandt clutched his shoulder. His arm felt dead.

It hung lifelessly at his side, pain shooting out from the joint, arching over his entire body.

Coach Hurley was at Brandt's side immediately. "I think you dislocated it," he said.

To Brandt's amazement, the coach firmly gripped Brandt's arm with both hands and shoved it back into place.

"Whoooooo!" Brandt cried in agony.

But the arm instantly felt better. The intense pain dulled to an ache.

"I've never seen anybody dislocate a shoulder that easily," Mr. Hurley said, scratching his bald head. "You ever pull the arm out before?"

"No," Brandt answered.

"Well, you'd better go to the nurse's office and get a sling," the coach told him. "You've got to get it X-rayed as soon as possible. I think your season may be over, son."

Out of the corner of his eye, Brandt saw Jon smirk.

Brandt turned away, forcing down his angry feelings, and trudged slowly out of the gym to find the nurse.

Half an hour later Brandt started walking home, moving awkwardly with his arm in a sling. "How am I going to explain this to Mom and Dad?" he asked himself. "A fistfight in the student senate?"

He crossed Park Drive and was halfway down the next block, when someone stepped out of the shadows and darted toward him.

Instinctively, Brandt backed away. "Stay away!" he shouted.

"Hey, Brandt, it's only me." A girl stepped into a pool of sunlight.

Meg.

"I know you didn't want to be my lab partner," she joked, "but I didn't think you were *terrified* of me!" She laughed her high-pitched, whistling laugh.

Brandt relaxed. "I'm sorry, Meg," he said. "It's been a long day."

Meg studied him curiously. "Hey—what happened to your arm?"

"Basketball practice," Brandt muttered. "I dislocated my shoulder."

Meg tossed back her auburn hair. "Jon didn't have anything to do with it—did he?" she asked suspiciously.

"No. Why?"

"I wanted to warn you about him," Meg said, her expression solemn. They started walking.

"What do you mean?" Brandt asked.

"Jon's a really intense guy," Meg warned. She plucked a twig from a tree as she walked. "You'll be sorry if you get on his bad side. He's got a terrible temper."

"I can handle that," Brandt said quietly.

"I'm serious, Brandt. He's real jealous when it comes to Jinny."

"Jinny and I are only lab partners," Brandt insisted.

"I know," Meg said. "But you don't know Jon. I mean, sometimes he goes ballistic. He got suspended from school last year for beating up a kid in Waynesbridge. The kid spent two weeks in the hospital."

She stopped at the corner. "Here's where I turn," she announced. A strand of auburn hair fell into her eyes. She made no move to brush it away.

"Thanks for the warning," Brandt told her. "But I think I can handle Jon."

Meg didn't reply. Instead, she completely startled Brandt by rising up on her toes and kissing him.

Quickly getting over his surprise, Brandt found himself kissing her back. She's really awesome, he told himself.

She stepped back and smiled at him. "I know you've got a study date with Jinny on Saturday," she said. "But why don't you come over to my house on Sunday? Not to study. We'll just—hang out."

"Sounds great," Brandt said. "See you then."

"See you." She flashed him another smile, shifted her backpack, and hurried away.

A few minutes later, still thinking about Meg, Brandt walked into his front yard. Abbie sat perched on a sagging front step, waiting for him. She was wearing her school uniform: a gray plaid skirt, white blouse, and blue sweater. She smiled and waved when she saw him.

Oh, wow! Brandt thought. As soon as he saw Abbie, he remembered—he had made a study date with her for Saturday. But now he had invited Jinny for Saturday afternoon too.

"How's it going, Brandt?" Abbie asked, climbing to her feet. "Hey—what happened to your arm?" Her blue eyes narrowed in concern.

"Just sprained it or something," Brandt replied, thinking about Saturday. "Uh—you know, Saturday—" he started.

"Would you like me to bring something? Some popcorn, maybe?" Abbie suggested. She gave him an eager smile.

"No, it's not that," Brandt said. "I—uh—got hung up Saturday. Some stuff I've got to do. Can we make it another day?"

Abbie's happy expression crumpled into disappointment. But she replied brightly, "Sure. Another day. No problem. Really."

She stood up quickly and started across the front lawn. "Catch you later," she called behind her.

"Right." Brandt watched her disappear around the hedges.

She'll get over it, he told himself.

He had to smile. Girls were throwing themselves at him right and left!

Maybe I'm going to like it here after all, he thought.

He turned and made his way into the house. "Mom—guess what?" he called. "You won't believe what a klutz I am! I fell down the stairs at school today!"

The doorbell rang at exactly two o'clock on Saturday afternoon. Brandt was sitting in the den, watching college football on TV.

He waited a minute until the first half of the game ended. Then he switched off the TV and went to answer the door.

His shoulder had nearly healed and he no longer needed the sling. But the coach refused to let him play basketball anymore.

I can live without basketball, Brandt thought. I've got plenty of other activities to keep me busy. Mainly, girls!

The doorbell rang again. Brandt fixed his smile, then pulled open the door.

Jinny gazed at him, fretfully chewing her bottom lip. She wore a maroon and white Shadyside High sweatshirt over black jeans. "This is your house?" she asked, raising her eyes to the peeling paint on the porch.

"Yeah," Brandt replied. "Pretty shabby, huh? We're fixing it up."

He stepped aside and let her in. Then he closed the door behind her. "Let me give you the grand tour. This is the dining room—"

He showed her the dark dining room, with its low, stained ceiling. In one corner the faded wallpaper was peeling off.

He pointed through a doorway and said, "There's the kitchen."

Jinny peered into the kitchen, which was more cheerful. "Where are your parents?" she asked.

"They went to a faculty tea in Waynesbridge," Brandt told her. "My dad teaches at the community college."

"Cool," Jinny said.

He led Jinny across the hall. "This is the living room."

The couch, a coffee table, and two chairs were surrounded by several half-unpacked cartons. Jinny walked over to the wall with Mr. McCloy's collection of weapons and armor.

"What *is* all this stuff?" she asked, lightly touching one of the darts.

"My father is an expert on ancient rituals," Brandt explained. "These are all things used in tribal warfare."

He pointed to a spear. "This is a really old spear that people used on the island in the Pacific where we lived," he said. "And these darts"—he touched the end of a brightly painted feathered dart—"are really deadly. They were used with a blowgun. The people on the island would blow them into the necks of their enemies. Their aim was so good, they always hit the jugular."

He paused, then urged, "Feel how sharp it is."

Jinny gingerly touched the point of the dart. "Ouch," she said, drawing back.

"That suit of armor," Brandt continued, "was also worn by the island warriors."

"Probably to protect themselves from the darts," Jinny joked.

Brandt watched as Jinny examined the armor. It was very heavy, made of iron, but securely fastened to the wall. The craftsman who made it had painted suns, moons, pyramids, and other symbols on the chestplate.

"I guess we'd better get started on our project," Jinny said, still eyeing the wall of weapons.

"Let's go up to my room," Brandt suggested. "I've got all my books and things up there."

They climbed the stairs to Brandt's room. Jinny sat at Brandt's desk. Brandt leaned across the desk to get a notebook.

Jinny tugged on the leather pouch he wore around his neck. "What's this?" she asked. "Some kind of weird change purse?"

Brandt tugged the pouch from her fingers. "It's a good-luck charm," he told her. "It saved my life once."

"How?"

Brandt hesitated. Why had he told her that? He really didn't feel like explaining it to her. He didn't like to talk about it.

"Never mind," he said, flashing her a smile. "You'll think I'm superstitious if I tell you."

"Whatever." Jinny shrugged.

Brandt picked up the chemistry textbook. "Have

72

you read through the list of experiments?" he asked.

Jinny nodded. "Which one do you want to do?"

"I haven't read the list yet," Brandt admitted, scanning the page.

"I'm kind of thirsty," Jinny said. "Do you mind if I go downstairs and get something to drink while you read the list?"

"No, go ahead," Brandt replied. "There's Coke and some other soda in the fridge."

"Do you want anything?" Jinny asked.

"No, thanks." He heard Jinny's footsteps as she descended the stairs.

She's really awesome, he thought, his eyes blurring over the words in his chemistry book.

Try to keep your mind on your book for five minutes, he scolded himself. She'll be annoyed if she comes back and you haven't even read the stupid list of experiments!

He was reading down the list when he heard her scream.

The book fell out of his hands.

"Jinny?"

Another shrill scream.

He raced out of the room, plunged down the stairs. Into the kitchen.

So much blood.

So much bright red blood.

Chapter 13

*B*randt's sneakers crunched over shards of broken glass as he crossed the room to Jinny.

"Make it stop!" she shrieked, her eyes wide with fear. "Make it stop—please!"

She raised both arms. Her hands were drenched with blood. The blood poured from her wrists, over her sweatshirt and jeans.

Brandt grabbed a dish towel off the counter and struggled to wrap it around one of Jinny's wrists.

"Make it stop! Make it stop!" she cried.

"We have to wrap both arms," he said, his eyes searching frantically for another towel.

"Make it stop! Make it stop!" Her eyes rolled wildly in her head. Somehow she had smeared blood over her face.

She's in shock, Brandt realized.

What on earth happened?

He jerked some paper towels off the roll and began wrapping them around the other wrist.

"Make it stop! Please—make it stop!" Her cries grew even shriller, more terrified.

As Brandt wrapped the towels tightly around Jinny's arms, his parents burst into the kitchen through the back door. With all the excitement, Brandt hadn't heard their car pull into the driveway.

"Oh, my!" Mrs. McCloy cried in alarm, raising her hands to her face. "What—"

She dropped her purse on the kitchen table and hurried to help Jinny. "Brandt! What's happened?"

"How did she cut herself?" Brandt's dad demanded.

"Make it stop! Make it stop!" Jinny shrieked.

Mrs. McCloy grabbed more paper towels and wrapped them tightly around Jinny's left arm.

"I'll get bandages." Mr. McCloy turned to hurry to the medicine chest.

"I—I don't know how it happened," Brandt stammered. Gazing down, he saw that his shirt and jeans were smeared with blood.

"The glass—it flew out of my hand!" Jinny screamed, her eyes finally starting to focus again. "It shattered in midair. I—I—I—"

Mrs. McCloy placed a comforting hand on Jinny's shoulder. "I think we're stopping the bleeding." She pulled back the paper towel and examined the wrist. "The cut isn't really that deep. You may not even need stitches."

"But the glass just flew!" Jinny cried, not seeming to hear Brandt's mother. "Like somebody pulled it away. And then it shattered. *For no reason!*"

Brandt gasped. He suddenly remembered Ezra. The spear had felt as if it were being pulled from Brandt's hand. And then it pierced the cat's body.

And now, the glass . . .

"Let's get you to the emergency room," Mrs. McCloy was saying, her arm still around Jinny's shoulders. "The bleeding has almost stopped. But we should have a doctor take a look at those cuts."

"It just shattered," Jinny repeated, still dazed. "It just shattered in midair."

The doctor at Shadyside Hospital bandaged Jinny's wrists. She didn't need stitches. She was feeling a little better by the time Brandt and his parents dropped her off at her house.

Brandt walked her up to the front door. "Great study date," she muttered, staring down at her bandages.

"Sorry," Brandt replied quietly.

"Next time, we'll study at *my* house," she said. She hurried inside.

Brandt's parents were waiting in the car. He told them he felt like walking home. "I really need to get some air."

"But you're covered in blood," Mrs. McCloy protested.

"It's a ten-minute walk," Brandt insisted. "I'll change as soon as I get home."

He watched them back down Jinny's drive and pull away. Then, shoving his hands into his jeans pockets, he began walking slowly toward home.

The late afternoon sky was low and gray. The air carried a damp chill.

He had turned the corner onto Fear Street, when out of the corner of his eye he thought he saw something move along a low hedge. He spun around.

No one there.

Brandt picked up his pace a little. The streetlights flickered on, casting shadows on the road.

Brandt suddenly felt sure that someone was following him. He stopped and listened.

Silence.

He turned back again.

A shadowy figure moved silently toward him.

Brandt shuddered. "No!" he cried. "Leave me alone!" He began to run.

The shadowy figure floated closer, moving silently, effortlessly, as if pushed forward on the wind.

Fear tightened Brandt's throat. "Go away!" he managed to choke out.

But the dark figure, all gray on shades of gray, slipped closer.

Closer.

Brandt forced his legs to run faster. He could see his house.

He felt a cold wind on his back. The icy touch of the shadowy stranger.

"No!" Brandt screamed shrilly. Using all his strength, he pulled away.

But the icy wind swept up his back.

His sneakers pounded on the sidewalk. He turned sharply. Into the tall grass of his front yard.

I'll be safe if I get to the house, he thought.

Safe from this cold, shadowy stranger.

Safe . . .

He tripped over a tree root. Stumbled to the ground.

Sprawled facedown in the tall, damp grass.

And waited in terror for the cold shadow to sweep over him.

Chapter 14

"Hey—Brandt?"

Brandt raised his head when he heard the voice.

"Brandt—are you okay?"

Abbie.

He spun around, his eyes searching the grass.

The shadow had vanished.

Who was it? *What* was it? He didn't have time to think about it. Abbie was making her way toward him over the tall grass, her expression showing her concern.

Embarrassed, Brandt climbed to his feet and brushed the dirt from his jeans. "I'm okay," he assured her. "I was running, and . . ." His voice trailed off.

"And you fell on your face?" She burst out laughing.

"Not funny," he muttered.

She covered her mouth and forced herself to stop. "Sorry. I saw you and—"

"Want to come in and talk for a while?" Brandt suggested.

Abbie glanced warily at the dark house. "To be honest, your house scares me a little."

"Let's just sit on the porch," he suggested.

She nodded and started to follow him. But she suddenly stopped and her expression changed. "What's that?" She pointed to the dark bloodstains on his sweater and jeans. "Is that mud?"

"Yeah. I guess," Brandt replied. He didn't feel like telling her the truth. "I'm such a klutz today."

"I have days like that," Abbie replied, eyeing him intently.

They settled on the porch steps. "Abbie," Brandt began thoughtfully, "what else do you know about this house? I mean, what else went on here before I moved in?"

"Hey, I'm not a snoopy neighbor," Abbie insisted. "I really don't know that much."

"Come on," Brandt coaxed. "You must have heard something—other weird stories. Or maybe you saw something strange going on."

Abbie shook her head. "I can't think of anything."

"What about the girl who died? Do you have any idea how it happened?"

Abbie wrinkled her nose. "Why are you asking me all these questions?"

Brandt realized that his questions were frightening Abbie—and that she couldn't help him. He suddenly wanted to be somewhere safe and warm. And he didn't want to be alone.

"Abbie," he began, trying to be casual about it. "Are you busy tonight? Maybe we could go see a movie."

"I wish I could," Abbie said. "But I can't go tonight. What about tomorrow afternoon?"

Brandt began to say yes, but he stopped himself. He remembered that he made a date with Meg.

"Tomorrow's no good. You sure you can't go out tonight?" he persisted. "We could see a comedy, a nice, cheerful movie where nobody dies or gets mutilated or anything."

Abbie laughed. "Sorry," she told him. "Another night."

"We just can't seem to get it together, can we?" Brandt complained.

"Hey, no problem," Abbie assured him. "We will. After all, we're neighbors." She stood up. "It's getting chilly. And dark. I'd better get home. See you later."

"See you."

As soon as Brandt opened the front door, his father called from the kitchen, "Is that you, Brandt?"

"Yes," Brandt replied.

"Get in here. Your mother and I want to talk to you."

Brandt ambled into the kitchen, taking his time. He wasn't looking forward to whatever his father had to say. He could tell by the tone of his voice that his father was unhappy about something.

Mrs. McCloy stood at the stove, stirring soup in a

large pot. Mr. McCloy was seated at the counter, chopping carrots for a salad.

The blood had all been washed up, Brandt saw happily.

When Brandt entered, Mr. McCloy set down his knife and raised his eyes to him. "Jinny seems like a nice girl," he said. "But your mother and I were a little surprised to find her here."

"We were working on our chemistry project. We're lab partners," Brandt answered curtly.

"Why didn't you tell us you'd invited her over, Brandt?" his mother asked, turning to face him. "Did you wait till we left and then invite her over?"

"No way," Brandt insisted impatiently. "I didn't know I had to tell you every little thing," Brandt answered. "I'm allowed to invite friends over— aren't I?"

His mother frowned, hurt. She turned back to the stove.

"We never mind if you have friends over," Mr. McCloy said. He changed his tone, trying to sound lighter, less upset. "It's just—well, we met your friend Abbie the other day, and then today it's Jinny. We don't think you should overdo it, that's all."

"Overdo what?" Brandt snapped, even though he knew perfectly well what they were talking about. He'd heard it before.

"You know," Mrs. McCloy said, "too many girls. It could be too much for you. Look what happened today. Jinny could have been seriously hurt."

"But that wasn't *my* fault!" Brandt protested. "It was an accident."

"We know that, Brandt," his father agreed. "But what if we hadn't come home when we did? It might have taken a lot out of you—"

"Give me a break. I can't take any more of this," Brandt muttered. "Call me when dinner's ready."

He stomped out of the kitchen.

Creak, creak, creak.

Brandt lay on his bed, staring up at the dark ceiling.

Creak, creak, creak.

The footsteps again. In the attic.

What did it mean? Who was up there? What was making those mysterious sounds?

Brandt decided to ignore them this time. He took a deep breath and closed his eyes.

Creak, creak, creak.

His eyes flew open. It was no use. He'd never be able to fall asleep. It sounded as if someone were pacing back and forth up there. Back and forth right over his bed.

One more time, he thought. I'm going to sneak up to that attic as quietly as I can.

This time maybe I'll catch whoever it is up there.

He slipped out of bed and crept up the attic stairs.

Silence.

He switched on the light. No one in view.

But there, in the middle of the floor, lay the diary.

It had been moved.

Brandt stepped toward it. The little book lay open.

Puzzled, Brandt bent down and picked up the diary.

"Huh?" He uttered a low cry when he saw the fresh writing.

A new page. Someone had started a new page.

His hand trembled and his eyes grew wide as he read the words, neatly written in blue ink.

> *I made Jinny bleed.*
> *Abbie is next.*

Chapter 15

Brandt dropped the diary as if it were burning hot.

I don't believe this! he thought.

His entire body trembled.

Who wrote the new entry? Who wrote these words?

He grabbed the diary and shuffled through the old pages. They were written in the same blue ink, he saw.

In the same handwriting.

Cally Frasier's handwriting!

But how could Cally Frasier still be writing in the diary? She was dead!

Still trembling, Brandt stared at the newly written words again.

> *I made Jinny bleed.*
> *Abbie is next.*

Such cold, cruel words.

Was it some kind of a joke? Brandt suddenly wondered. Was someone trying to scare him?

No.

No one else had been up in the attic. No one.

So what did it mean?

Was the house really haunted? Haunted by the ghost of Cally Frasier?

Had a ghost written these frightening new words?

Had a ghost killed Ezra and cut Jinny?

And was the ghost really planning to hurt Abbie next?

Brandt shut the diary and tossed it against the wall.

He suddenly remembered the shadowlike figure that had chased him onto the front yard. *That* was the ghost! he decided.

The ghost was outside. It chased me home. The ghost is outside—and inside the house.

This is crazy, he thought. Totally crazy.

He climbed to his feet. But if it is for real, I can stop it, he told himself. Whatever it is, whoever it is—I won't let Abbie get hurt.

"I know there's evil in this house," he whispered, wondering if the ghost could hear him. "But if anyone can beat it, I can."

Brandt woke up early and hurried to the phone to warn Abbie.

He held the receiver in his hand—and realized he didn't know her number. Or her last name.

Didn't she tell me her last name? He struggled to remember.

He put down the phone and hurried to the front door. Stepping out into a blustery gray morning that threatened rain, he made his way down the driveway.

Which house is hers? he wondered, turning first to the left, then to the right. Or did Abbie say she lived across the street?

The houses all looked dark. It was a little after eight o'clock, but no lights were on in any of them.

I *have* to warn Abbie, Brandt told himself. She'll probably think I'm crazy. But I have to warn her.

As he turned and trudged back into the house, he vowed to tell her the next time he saw her. If I have to, I'll search door to door, he decided.

I won't let Abbie get hurt. I won't.

"That's the weirdest thing I ever heard," Meg said.

Brandt had just told her about the diary. He *had* to tell someone. And Meg had proven to be a good listener.

She was sitting with her legs tucked under her on a low chair in her den. Brandt sat cross-legged on the floor, leaning back against the couch.

Brandt yawned for the hundredth time. He was exhausted from being awake the entire night. But he hadn't wanted to cancel his date with Meg.

Meg had rented a movie. She'd pressed the Pause

button and stood up to get more popcorn, when she noticed how tired Brandt looked. "Are you okay?" she had asked him.

That's when he had told her about the footsteps in the attic—and about Cally Frasier's diary.

"Someone is playing a really mean joke on you," Meg said. "What else could it be?"

"But who would do it? And how are they doing it?" Brandt wondered aloud. "And why? It doesn't make sense."

Meg stared at him, thinking hard. "I'll bet it's Jon," she said finally.

Brandt laughed. "You always want to blame Jon for everything."

Meg looked hurt. "I'm being serious." She shoved a strand of auburn hair off her forehead. "You don't know Jon. He's jealous of you, Brandt. He—"

"Jon may be very slick on the basketball court. But he isn't slick enough to sneak up into my attic and write in Cally Frasier's handwriting," Brandt told her firmly.

Meg settled back on the chair, frowning.

The closet door suddenly moved with a squeak.

Brandt gasped, staring at the door in terror.

"It's only Lulu," Meg told him. A fluffy white cat slinked out of the closet and settled onto Meg's lap. "Whoa. You're awfully jumpy today."

Brandt let out a long, slow breath. I keep expecting shadowy ghosts to jump out at me wherever I go, he thought.

I can't ever let my guard down for a second.

He decided not to tell Meg about the choking

cloud of white smoke that burst from his closet. Or the shadowy ghost that chased him home.

She'll think I'm a total psycho! he told himself.

And then, a troubling thought—*Maybe I am.*

Meg set the cat down, crossed the room, and sat down on the floor next to Brandt. "Relax," she said softly. "Let's think about something else for a while."

She leaned forward and kissed him.

Brandt wrapped his arms around her and kissed her too. Her lips were soft and warm. He wanted to be kissed. He needed to be kissed. He pressed his mouth against hers hungrily.

"Hey!" Something jabbed his leg. Something sharp.

Brandt cried out and pulled away from Meg. "What was that?"

Meg reached behind him and pulled Lulu into her arms. "The stupid cat," she told him. "Did she claw you? Sorry."

Brandt smiled tensely. "Oh." He started to pull her close to kiss her again.

But the front doorbell rang.

Meg sighed. "I'll be right back." She climbed to her feet and made her way across the living room to the front door. Brandt could see the door from where he sat on the den floor.

"Hey, Megster." Brandt recognized Jinny's voice.

Uh-oh, Brandt thought, straightening his hair with his fingers. He moved from the floor to the couch, hoping that position would seem more— innocent.

Jinny, in dark green jeans and a pale yellow sweater, strode into the house, Meg at her heels. "I just stopped by for a second to—"

When she spotted Brandt on the couch, her mouth dropped open in surprise. Her face turned red, but she recovered quickly. "Oh. Hi, Brandt. What are *you* doing here?"

"We're just studying," Meg replied for him.

"With no books?" Jinny's voice grew shrill. Her eyes fell on the TV and she added, "While watching a movie?"

"Want to join us?" Brandt asked lightly. He patted the couch cushion next to him.

"Uh—Meg, could I see you for a minute in the next room?" Jinny demanded. It wasn't really a question.

Meg followed Jinny into the living room. Brandt could hear them whispering sharply, angrily, to each other.

"Hey, don't fight over me, girls!" he called, trying to keep it light. "There's plenty of me to go around!"

They ignored him and kept whispering. A few seconds later Brandt heard the front door slam.

Meg returned to the den, her cheeks bright pink. "What's Jinny's problem anyway?" she demanded. "She already *has* a boyfriend!"

Brandt left Meg's house a short while later. Jinny's appearance had spoiled the afternoon. Brandt liked the idea of having two girls fight over him. But he was too exhausted and stressed out to be able to deal with it then.

His parents were out when he got home. The house sat quiet and dark, mysterious and full of secrets.

Brandt hesitated for a second, feeling weary, worn out—and frightened. Taking a deep breath, he walked up the stairs and straight to the attic.

He had to see the diary.

Would it be where he left it? Would there be any new entries?

He stepped onto the attic floor. A dim shaft of light filtered through the attic window, casting a halo of dust around the diary.

Brandt knelt beside the book. With trembling fingers he opened the cover. Then he turned to the last page.

Was there a new entry?

He raised the open diary, read the last page— and gasped in horror.

Chapter 16

> *I made Jinny bleed.*
> *Abbie is next.*
> *Brandt, you cannot save Abbie.*

"No!" Brandt cried out loud. He slammed the diary shut and squeezed the book in his hand, squeezed it until his hand ached.

"Cally Frasier—can you hear me?" he called.

Silence.

"Are you writing these threats in your diary, Cally?" Brandt demanded in a quivering voice.

Silence.

"I'm taking your diary away!" he shouted. "I'm taking it and hiding it, Cally! So you can't make any more threats!"

He moved quickly to the stairs, the diary still clasped tightly in his hand.

Have I gone totally crazy? he asked himself. Am I really up here shouting at a ghost?

He clamored heavily down the stairs.

Into his room.

If there is no diary, will the evil still happen? he wondered.

Can I save Abbie by hiding the diary?

He glanced around the room, desperately searching for a hiding place.

The closet?

No. He remembered that green glow, the flash of white that had sprung out at him from the closet.

The diary wouldn't be safe there.

He pulled open his bottom dresser drawer and tossed the diary under a stack of T-shirts. It would have to do.

As he pushed the drawer closed, Brandt heard a voice.

"Mom? Dad?" he called. "Are you home?"

No answer.

He hurried to the window and checked the driveway. No. No sign of his parents.

He heard the voice again. Tiny. Far away.

"Cally? Is that you? Did you come to find your diary?" he demanded, his eyes searching the room.

A muffled voice. Out in the hall.

He stepped out into the hallway and listened.

Crying? Was someone crying?

"Hello?" he called. "Is someone here?"

The muffled cry grew louder. A whimpering dog? A child?

But where? Where was it coming from?

Gripped with fear, Brandt forced his legs to carry

93

him down the dimly lit hall. The tiny cries seemed to come from an empty bedroom. He stopped outside the door to the room and listened. "Is anybody in there? Can you hear me?"

As he stepped into the empty room, he heard the little boy's frightened voice. "Mommy, it's me! Are you there, Mommy?"

"Wh-who is it?" Brandt stammered. "Where are you?"

"Help me, Mommy! Help me! Come get me, Mommy. It's so dark here. Come get me! It's me—James!"

Chapter 17

The little boy's tiny, terrified voice sent a cold shudder down Brandt's spine.

"Mommy! Mommy! Where are you?" the voice cried. "Come get me, Mommy! Please!"

Brandt switched on the light. A single bare bulb shone in a ceiling fixture.

His eyes darted frantically around the room. No one there.

"Mommy!" the voice pleaded. "Help me! Come get me! It's so dark here!"

No, Brandt thought. It's impossible.

The voice seemed to be coming from inside the wall.

Brandt froze, unable to decide what to do. Taking a deep breath, he forced himself to the wall and pressed his hands against it.

95

Was there some kind of trapdoor in the wall? Some kind of secret compartment? He ran his hands all along the wall, pressing hard. But it was solid—plaster.

"Take me home, Mommy! It's James! Mommy, where are you?"

James. James. Why does that name sound familiar? Brandt asked himself.

The diary, he remembered. Cally wrote about her brother, a little boy named James. She told a horrifying story. About how James and his dog disappeared—and were never found.

But Cally's family heard James calling to them. Calling from inside the walls.

Could that little boy still be alive? Brandt wondered, staring at the white plaster wall.

No. It was impossible. The house had been empty for more than a year.

"Mommy, I'm scared! It's so dark in here! I'm so lonely! Get me out, Mommy!"

"I'll help you, James!" Brandt shouted. "Don't be afraid. I'll help you!"

But how?

Somehow he had to open up the wall.

"Please don't leave me, Mommy! Don't leave me behind!"

"Don't worry, James," Brandt called. "I'll be right back."

He hurried downstairs and frantically rummaged through the cartons stacked in the dining room. He knew his father had packed his tools somewhere.

A few minutes later he returned to the room, carrying a large wooden mallet.

"James?" Brandt called. "Are you still here?"

"Mommy! Get me out!" the boy screeched.

"All right," Brandt called in a soothing voice. "Wherever you are, James, step away from this side of the wall."

Brandt waited a few seconds. Then he heaved the mallet and swung it at the wall. It cracked a hole in the plaster.

Brandt peered inside the hole.

Nothing but darkness. No sign of the boy.

"James?" Brandt called.

Silence.

Then, "Mommy! I want to come back! Please, Mommy?"

"Hold on, James!" Brandt called breathlessly. He raised the heavy mallet—and swung again. Again. Again.

The plaster crumbled. The hole widened.

Brandt struggled to catch his breath. A sour odor invaded his nostrils. He recognized it at once—the same stench he'd smelled in his room a few days before.

The stench of decay, of rotting flesh.

One more swing of the mallet, and the wall fell away.

"Ohhhhh." Brandt uttered a sickened cry. The mallet dropped from his hands and landed at his feet with a thud.

He was staring at the most gruesome sight he had ever seen in his life.

Chapter 18

As Brandt gaped in horror, the skeleton of a child toppled out of the wall. The child's bony hands clutched a dog's skeleton in its arms.

Holding his breath against the foul odor, Brandt forced himself to look. The small body was decomposed.

A ragged little pair of jeans and a shirt clung to the boy's bones.

The bones tumbled in a heap to the floor.

Brandt turned away, fighting down his nausea.

The room lay in silence now. The pitiful cries had stopped.

Brandt stared at the hideous little skull with its patch of red hair. This boy was calling to me, Brandt knew. That was the tiny voice that I heard.

But how?

Abbie's words echoed in his mind. *The house is evil.*

The house is evil.

Maybe, Brandt thought.

Or maybe the house was haunted—by the ghost of James.

Brandt's parents returned home about an hour after Brandt discovered the skeleton.

Mrs. McCloy gasped in horror at the sight. But Brandt's father stared at the two skeletons, fascinated. "This could explain a lot of strange things about the house," he told Brandt. "The noises you've been hearing, your sense that someone's in the room with you—" He paused.

"It's not a classic case," he mused. "But I think we've had a poltergeist."

"What are we going to do with these bones?" Mrs. McCloy moaned. "How can you be talking about poltergeists when we have the skeleton of a child on our floor?"

"Poltergeists are often the ghosts of children," Mr. McCloy continued, staring at the pile of bones. "They're mischievous, but they rarely hurt anyone. No one has been hurt in this house, have they?"

"What about Jinny?" Brandt demanded. "And what about poor Ezra?"

"Hmmmm." Mr. McCloy rubbed his chin thoughtfully.

"Mischievous doesn't describe what I've felt in this house," Brandt said heatedly. "It's more like—evil."

"That's just because it scares you," Mr. McCloy insisted. "Because you don't know what causes it, it seems mysterious."

A heavy silence fell over the room as the three of them stared at the skeleton of James and the dog.

Poor kid, Brandt thought. He sounded so frightened, so alone.

How did he get trapped in the wall?

And how could he be calling out to us more than a year after he died?

Brandt's head spun with questions. So many questions.

Mr. McCloy broke the silence.

"We'd better call the police. They will deal with the remains. And get in touch with the family."

As they made their way downstairs, Mr. McCloy put an arm around Brandt's shoulder. "Maybe the house will settle down now," he said. "Once this poor boy is buried and can rest in peace."

Brandt sighed. "I hope so, Dad. I really do."

Poor James, the ghost of Cally thought as she watched the grim-faced police officers carry away her brother's bones.

My poor brother James.

You were such a cute little guy. So sweet. So beautiful.

And look at you now.

"Oh!" An officer uttered a cry as his hand slipped and the dog's skull clattered to the floor. It rolled to a stop at Cally's feet.

She floated back.

Goodbye, James, she thought. Goodbye. I hope you rest better than me.

She realized she felt no sadness. Her anger was much too strong to allow any soft feelings in.

Too late, James, she thought, feeling her bitterness surge.

Too late for you. Too late for me.

She floated close to Brandt, who stood watching the police officers go about their unpleasant job.

Don't get too cozy, Brandt, Cally told him silently. Because your problems aren't over yet.

It's too late for James. Too late for me.

And—it's too late for you.

Chapter 19

On Saturday morning Brandt stepped outside to get the newspaper. He opened the front door to find Abbie standing on the porch, ready to ring the bell.

"Hi," she said brightly.

"Hey—Abbie!" Brandt cried in surprise. "You're looking good!"

She was cute in a pair of faded jeans, a white shirt, and a pale blue vest.

Abbie smiled. "What's up?"

Brandt leaned down and picked up the folded newspaper. "Not much. Why don't you come in?"

He suddenly pictured the warning in the diary: *Abbie is next.* Should he warn her about it?

No, he decided. The threat is all gone. The little

boy's bones had been removed nearly a week before. And nothing strange or frightening had happened in the house since then.

No need to scare Abbie, Brandt decided. No need to make her think I'm some kind of paranoid nutcase.

She followed him inside. Brandt stepped into the kitchen to give the newspaper to his mother. She was washing the breakfast dishes.

He found Abbie in the living room, staring at his father's wall of old weapons.

"What's all this stuff?" she asked. "It's so strange and primitive looking."

"This is my dad's collection of arms and armor," Brandt explained. "He's really into old tribal weapons and stuff."

"How did he get it all?" Abbie asked. She stared at the thin, feathered darts in fascination. "Did he buy them?"

"No. We lived on a remote island in the Pacific for a couple of years," Brandt told her. "The people there were into weird stuff. They had all kinds of bizarre customs and ceremonies."

"Like what?" Abbie asked.

Brandt paused, remembering. "Well, they used a lot of weird herbs to mix love potions and things like that. They believed in spirits and ghosts."

"Wow," Abbie said. "It must have been cool to live there."

"It was interesting," Brandt admitted. "But it was difficult too. They thought differently from us.

Like, they believed every animal and person has two spirits, not just one."

"You mean like split personalities?"

"No," Brandt explained. "One spirit is your personality. It's what makes you different from other people. And the other spirit is a sort of life force that keeps you alive. That's why they sacrifice animals and drink the blood."

"I don't get it," Abbie said.

"They think the blood contains the animal's life force—and if they drink it, their own life force will get stronger."

"And what happens to the other spirit—the personality spirit?" Abbie asked.

"That becomes your ghost. Your personality spirit can haunt people if it wants to."

Abbie stared at the wall thoughtfully. "Did you ever see a ghost while you were there?" she asked.

"No," Brandt replied. "No, I never did."

Abbie stepped closer to the wall, examining a spear. Brandt heard the telephone ring in the kitchen. A moment later his mother called, "Brandt! Phone!"

"I'll be right back," he told Abbie. He hurried into the kitchen. His mother handed him the phone and stepped away, wiping down a counter.

"Hello?"

"Hi, Brandt. It's Jinny."

Brandt couldn't hide his surprise. "Jinny—hi!" he exclaimed. "I haven't talked to you all week. I thought maybe—"

THE SECOND HORROR

Brandt didn't get to finish his sentence. A loud, clattering crash from the living room interrupted him.

He dropped the phone receiver when he heard the chilling scream.

Abbie's scream.

Chapter 20

Abbie's screams rose shrilly.

Brandt cried out in surprise and raced out of the kitchen.

"Abbie?" He found her on the floor, pinned under the heavy suit of armor.

"Help me!" Abbie cried. "I can't move!"

"Oh, my goodness!" Mrs. McCloy cried, right behind Brandt. "How did this happen?"

Brandt struggled to lift the metal suit off Abbie. "It—it won't budge!" he stammered.

Abbie moaned and tried to move one of her arms. "Hurry," she pleaded. "I can't breathe. It's so heavy."

Brandt struggled to lift the armor. His mother stepped to the other side and bent to help. They managed to move it just enough for Abbie to wriggle out from under it.

"Are you all right?" Brandt asked. "Does anything feel broken?"

Abbie remained seated on the floor, her expression dazed. She rubbed her arm. "It—it just flew off the wall," she murmured. "I was looking at it—and it flew off the wall. It didn't just fall, Brandt. It *flew!*"

"It was hanging very securely," Mrs. McCloy said, puzzled. "I know we checked the hooks three times. Nothing like this has happened before."

Brandt helped Abbie to her feet. He led her to the couch. Mrs. McCloy hurried to the kitchen to get her a glass of water.

Brandt sat down beside Abbie. "I don't know how to tell you this," he began. "But someone knew that you would have an accident. Someone predicted it."

"Huh?" Abbie sat up straight. "Who? Who predicted it?"

"I don't know," Brandt replied uneasily. "One of the twins who used to live here—her name was Cally—kept a diary. I found it in the attic. But sometimes when I look at it—" He hesitated.

"What?" Abbie asked. "Go on, Brandt."

"There are new entries," Brandt told her. "I know it sounds crazy. But someone is still writing in it. And the last entry predicted that you would get hurt."

"I told you this house was evil!" Abbie exclaimed, close to tears.

Brandt put his arms around her, trying to calm her. "It could have been an accident," he said in a soothing voice, though he didn't believe it himself. "Or just a coincidence."

"It wasn't," Abbie declared. "I know it wasn't."

"Anyway, you're okay," Brandt said. "You weren't really hurt, right?"

Abbie sniffed. "I guess not. But someone *will* get hurt here, Brandt. The stories about this house must be true."

Brandt held his arms around her but said nothing.

It could have been an accident, he told himself again.

James is buried. The ghost is gone.

The house is no longer haunted.

Right?

Brandt sat up as the bell rang, ending school. He rubbed his eyes. Then slowly followed the other kids out of the classroom.

Well, I made it through another day, he thought. But if I don't get some sleep soon, I'll start dozing off in class.

He had spent another sleepless night. The footsteps in the attic had returned. He lay staring up at the ceiling, gripping the blankets tightly, listening. Listening all night.

With a weary sigh, he stood at his locker, daydreaming. He heard a basketball being bounced on the hard floor.

"McCloy. I want to talk to you."

Brandt raised his eyes to discover Jon Burks beside him. "Listen, Jon," Brandt said, "I don't have much time—"

Jon tucked the basketball under one arm and placed his other hand on Brandt's shoulder. "What's up, man?" he asked, grinning at Brandt.

"Not much," Brandt replied, edging away. "I've got to get going, Jon." Glancing down the hall, Brandt noticed that all the other kids had left.

"How's the bad shoulder?" Jon asked, ignoring Brandt's impatience. He slapped the shoulder. "How's that feel? Not too bad?" His grin remained frozen on his face.

"See you later," Brandt uttered. He turned and headed away.

But Jon kept up with him. "Hey, what's up with you and Jinny?"

Brandt stopped short. "Why don't you ask *her?*" he snapped.

Jon's face turned bright red. He leaned menacingly toward Brandt. "Don't mess with me," he muttered. He bumped Brandt's shoulder hard.

Brandt knew he should back away. But he never could take the easy way out. "Watch out for those fouls, Jon," he said sharply.

Jon's face turned even redder. "Jinny and you— it isn't going to happen," he said softly. He bounced the ball against the wall, just missing Brandt's head. Then he bounced it again. "You've got to remember one thing," he told Brandt, his grin returning. "You bruise real easily."

Brandt didn't reply. His eyes were staring over Jon's shoulder. He saw something in the empty hall.

A dark shape.

A shadow.

It hovered behind Jon. Jon seemed unaware of the presence behind him. But Brandt saw it. He gaped at it in terror.

It's back, Brandt realized. Whoever it is— whatever it is—it's following me.

Jon's threats meant nothing to Brandt now. He sensed that the shadow figure was far more dangerous than Jon could ever be.

I can't let Jon leave me, Brandt thought. I've got to stick with him until this thing goes away.

"Maybe you bruise easily too," he told Jon. "Want to find out? Want to see who bruises the most easily?"

Jon's eyes widened in surprise. "Huh? No way, man. I mean, no way. I'm not fighting you. I don't want a slaughter on my hands."

"Hey, don't wimp out," Brandt challenged. "Come on, Jon. Let's go. Right here."

Brandt shoved Jon's shoulder. Jon barely moved. He just stared back at Brandt, amazed. "Get serious," Jon muttered.

Brandt shoved him again.

"You don't know what you're doing," Jon warned. "You can't fight me."

"You scared?" Brandt demanded. "You *chicken*, Jon?"

Jon brushed Brandt's arm away. He shook his head. "You're the weirdest guy I ever met," he said. He turned and started down the hall.

Brandt panicked. The shadowy figure loomed up behind Jon.

"Jon—wait!" Brandt called desperately. "You going to basketball practice?"

Jon kept walking. He didn't reply.

Brandt glanced at the dark shadow, moving closer—and hurried to catch up to Jon. "I think I'll come along and watch," he said. "How's the team surviving without me?"

Jon stared at him as if he were insane. "You've got problems, McCloy," he said, rolling his eyes. "Major problems."

I know, Brandt thought, glancing back. The shadowy figure gave up then, retreating around the corner.

What is it? Brandt wondered, breathing a sigh of relief. Why is it following me?

How long will I be able to avoid it?

Chapter 21

The diary.

The diary has the answers, Brandt thought.

He had stuck close to Jon all the way to the gym, afraid the shadowy figure would be waiting outside the school.

But it wasn't. It had vanished. Brandt had run all the way home.

I've got to do something, Brandt told himself, slamming the door behind him and locking it. I've got to do something—before it gets me. Before it tries to hurt Abbie again.

He shut himself up in his room. He furiously read through Cally's diary, searching for clues, for hints, for anything that could help explain the dark ghost to him.

Cally seemed so nice in the beginning, he thought

sadly as he paged through the diary. Funny. Fun to be with.

I would have liked her. I know I would have.

But what happened to her?

Is she really dead? Is she the ghost haunting this house? Is she the one writing the new entries and hurting my friends?

Is Cally the dark shadow that has been following me?

Questions. Nothing but questions. No answers.

Brandt shut the diary and carried it across the hall to his father's study.

Bookshelves lined the study walls, but half of them stood empty. Unopened cartons were piled on the floor.

Brandt scanned the bookshelves, looking for a title that might help him. He saw dusty, ancient volumes written in languages he didn't recognize. Mr. McCloy collected antique books on spells and strange rites.

"No good, no good, no good," Brandt murmured, reading the spines of the books. "If only I could read Latin."

He gave up on the books on the shelves and ripped open a carton.

He pulled out books called *Reincarnation in Ancient Egypt, The Occult in San Francisco,* and *Poisons, Potions, and the Sumerian Gods.* Shaking his head, he stacked them on the floor.

At last he found a book that interested him: *The Nature of Evil.* He scanned its pages, searching for anything that might answer his questions.

"Evil never dies," the author wrote. "Those who do its work can be conquered. But evil itself never goes away. It only seeks a new vessel.

"Anyone can become a victim of evil. Even the kindest heart, the gentlest soul, is at its mercy."

That's what happened to Cally Frasier, Brandt thought.

Something evil got her—and changed her.

Something in this house.

He thought of the attic. The creaking. The footsteps.

The attic had things the Frasiers had left behind in their hurry to leave. Maybe they left behind a clue, he thought.

A clue about what happened to Cally. About how I can keep the same thing from happening to me.

Clutching the diary, he hurried to the attic.

He switched on the light. The bare bulb cast harsh shadows around the room.

Brandt frantically began digging through the Frasiers' dusty boxes. He found children's books, a teddy bear with one eye missing, old clothes.

Then he came across a photograph in a wooden frame. He picked it up in a trembling hand. The glass was cracked, the picture slightly faded.

It showed two blond girls about twelve or thirteen standing together in front of an apartment building. The girls were smiling and had their arms wrapped around each other. A little red-haired boy stood in front of them, grinning. One of his front teeth was missing.

Sisters. Twin sisters. And their younger brother.

A picture of Cally, Kody, and James.

It was taken before they moved here, Brandt figured. They seemed so happy.

Before all the trouble. Before their family was ripped apart. Before James and Cally died.

He dropped the photo back into the box.

It won't happen to me, he vowed silently.

It won't happen to Abbie or Jinny or Meg. I won't let it.

A noise cut through the silence.

Brandt tensed. What was that?

It sounded like a giggle.

Brandt strained to hear. Laughter. Soft laughter. A girl's laughter.

Where was it coming from? Downstairs?

He hurried down the attic stairs and stood in the second floor hallway.

The laughter grew louder. He spun around. It seemed to surround him.

"Hey!" he cried. "Who's there? Where are you?"

Such cold laughter. So joyless. Scornful laughter. Louder. And shrill. Screeching.

Harsh and unpleasant laughter. Evil laughter.

"Where are you? Who is here?" he cried.

Covering his ears with his hands, he ran from room to room, frantically searching for the laughing girl. "Stop it! Stop!" he shouted.

Covering his ears didn't help. The cruel laughter rang out as if inside his head. Louder. Louder. The laughter of a girl gone mad.

Trying to escape the frightening sound, Brandt lunged into his room and slammed the door. The harsh, grating laughter followed him, swirled around him, louder, louder.

"Stop it! Please—I can't *stand* it!" He couldn't hear his own cries over the roar of laughter.

He turned on the radio. The sound of a heavy metal group blared out. He cranked the volume up all the way.

But the laughter pounded in his ears, louder than the loudest music.

"Stop! *Stop!*"

Louder and louder, it echoed and rang—until Brandt's entire body throbbed with pain.

My head is going to split open! Brandt realized. The laughter—it's going to kill me!

Chapter 22

Brandt threw open his bedroom door and ran out into the hall. The laughter and thudding music followed him as he scrambled down the stairs.

Got to get away. Got to get out!

He pulled open the front door. And raced out of the house. He didn't stop running until he reached the street.

His ears rang. His body throbbed and vibrated as if he had received a powerful electrical shock.

But the laughter had stopped.

He had escaped.

Struggling to catch his breath, waiting for the ringing in his ears to fade, he stared across the dark yard at the house.

Can I go back inside? he wondered.

What is waiting in there for me next?

The ghost of Cally Frasier watched Brandt from the upstairs window. A cruel smile played over her pale face as she watched him stagger into the street, holding his ears.

What's wrong, Brandt? she asked silently. Don't you like to hear a girl having fun?

I'll bet you like it when Jinny laughs. And Meg. And Abbie.

Why not me?

Cally sighed. These silly pranks were losing their excitement, she decided. It was too easy to frighten Brandt. Too boring.

Brandt and I are going to spend a long, long time together, she knew. It will be much more fun when Brandt is dead too.

She watched him staring up at the house.

It will be better when we can laugh together, Brandt, she told him silently. I'm getting so impatient.

First I'll take care of your friends.

And then I'll take care of you.

Chapter 23

*B*randt jumped when the doorbell rang on Wednesday afternoon after school. He wasn't expecting anyone.

His mother had gone shopping, and his father was sawing some branches off a tree in the side yard. Mr. McCloy didn't teach on Wednesdays.

The doorbell rang again. Brandt stepped quietly to the front window and peered out.

Jinny and Meg.

Brandt opened the door. The two girls smiled at him. Meg held a plate covered with aluminum foil in her hands. "Happy birthday!" Jinny cried, laughing.

"It's not my birthday," Brandt told them.

"Of course it is," Jinny insisted. She handed him the plate.

"It's brownies," Meg explained. "We had some left over from the bake sale last week. We thought you'd like them."

"They're not *too* stale," Jinny added. "Only a little."

"But it's not my birthday," Brandt insisted.

"That's why we didn't bring a cake!" Meg exclaimed.

Both girls burst out laughing.

Jinny's expression turned serious. "We heard about Jon getting on your case the other day," she said. "I'm sorry about that."

"No problem," Brandt replied. "Actually, I got on *his* case."

"We know," Jinny said. "He told us he didn't want to hurt you. He's not such a jerk after all, I guess."

"Jinny likes him again," Meg explained.

"Shut up!" Jinny shot back, shoving Meg off the porch.

"Come on in," Brandt urged. "You can have a stale brownie."

The girls exchanged glances. Brandt caught the fear in their eyes.

"Hey—you're not scared, are you?" Brandt teased.

Jinny held up her hands. The wrists had tiny scars. "I haven't recovered from the last time I was here!" she exclaimed.

"Come on, Jinny," Meg prompted. "Just for a couple of minutes. Really, what could happen?"

"Okay," Jinny replied tensely. "I—I kind of decided . . . That is, my mother convinced me . . .

You know, that thing with the glass. It must have been an accident, right? I mean, what else could have happened?"

Brandt stepped aside to let the girls in. "We'll all be real careful this time," he said. He nearly dropped the plate of brownies—and they all laughed.

He led them into the living room. The McCloys had unpacked more of the cartons, and the room looked a little more lived-in.

Brandt set the plate on the coffee table and pulled off the tinfoil. Outside the window, he could hear his father sawing at a branch.

"Help yourselves to the brownies," he offered.

"We don't want them," Meg said. "That's why we brought them over in the first place. So we wouldn't eat them all."

"I sort of want one," Jinny admitted. She took a brownie and nibbled on it. Then she wandered over to the wall and fingered one of the brightly colored darts.

"Did you ever see these, Meg?" Jinny asked.

"No," Meg replied. "What are they?"

"They're deadly darts," Jinny told her. "Right, Brandt?"

"Right," Brandt replied. "You shoot them with a blowgun." Brandt scanned the wall for a blowgun to show them. Then he went to a table in a corner of the room and pulled open a drawer.

"Here's a blowgun." Brandt pulled a short wooden tube from the drawer. "I guess it's okay if I show it to you."

He glanced out the window at his father. Mr.

McCloy was still working away. He didn't seem to be making much progress.

Jinny took the tube and examined it. It was hollow, made of dark brown wood, and painted with interesting red and yellow symbols.

"These red marks stand for death," Brandt explained. "I think the yellow symbols have something to do with reincarnation."

"And they kill people with this?" Jinny asked. "Amazing. It's so small."

"Want me to show you how it works?" Brandt asked.

The girls nodded.

Brandt carefully picked a dart from the wall. "You place the dart in this slot," he said, sliding the dart into a niche at one end of the tube. "Make sure the point is going in the right direction. And make sure you don't *inhale!*"

The girls laughed.

"You put your lips at this end and blow." Brandt puffed a small amount of air, pretending to blow through the gun.

"You must have to blow hard to get the dart to go far enough," Meg said.

"The island people know some kind of trick for that," Brandt explained. "They can give just a little puff, and the dart flies out hundreds of feet. It's amazing."

"Brandt!" Mr. McCloy called from outside.

Brandt hurried to the window. His father was sweating from his effort. But the branch he was working on still clung to the dead tree. "Can you come out and help me a minute?" he shouted.

Brandt nodded at him and turned back to the girls. "I'll be right back," he said.

"I hope we don't eat all the brownies while you're gone," Jinny said, picking up a second one.

Brandt pulled on a sweater and hurried out the door to help his father.

"Check this out, Brandt," Mr. McCloy said fretfully. "Did you ever see wood like this before?"

Brandt examined the cut his father had made in the branch. The wood wasn't gray-brown, as dead wood should be, but dark red. Like blood.

"What kind of tree is this?" Brandt asked.

"I have no idea," his father admitted. "If I had to make up a name for it, I'd call it a bloodwood tree. It's the toughest wood I've ever tried to cut. I wonder how it will burn."

Brandt took the saw from his father and pulled it across the branch a few times. He managed to cut the branch halfway through.

"We're getting there," his father said. He took back the saw and worked some more, groaning with every movement. Finally, the branch cracked and fell to the ground. Bright red sap oozed from the branch's cut surface.

"Weird," Brandt exclaimed. "The sap really does look like blood."

"It does, doesn't it," Mr. McCloy agreed. "You know, I've had enough of this. I'm going to call Mr. Hankers and see if he can do anything with these trees. I'm getting too old for this. And you—"

His father stopped, but Brandt knew what he was thinking.

My condition, he thought with irritation. I shouldn't be chopping trees with my condition.

"You can go back inside now if you want," Mr. McCloy said. "I'm going to clean up the mess I've made."

"All right." Brandt walked around to the kitchen door.

"Hey, Jinny, Meg!" Brandt called from the hall. "I hope you saved a brownie for me!"

No reply.

That's strange, he thought. Those two never shut up when they're together.

Maybe they got bored waiting for me and left, Brandt thought, a little disappointed.

"Meg? Jinny?" he called as he walked toward the living room.

Still no reply.

Brandt stepped into the living room. "Hey!"

He saw the blowgun on the floor.

And lying a few feet away were Meg and Jinny.

Their eyes were open, staring, blank. Their mouths hung open in frozen horror.

Each girl had a dart stuck in her throat.

Chapter 24

"They're lucky to be alive," Dr. Morgan said.

Brandt and his father stood listening in the emergency waiting room at the hospital. The doctor, a tall, middle-aged woman with short brown hair, had removed the darts from Meg's and Jinny's throats. She tucked her hands into the pockets of her white lab coat as she spoke to the girls' parents.

"They'll both have to stay here at least several days," Dr. Morgan went on. "They seem to have some minor nerve damage and they are in shock. Neither girl has regained consciousness yet."

"But will they be okay?" Jinny's mother asked. "I mean, when they wake up?"

The doctor sighed. "We have no way of knowing," she replied softly. "But they should make a full recovery. They should be fine."

A short while later Mr. McCloy led Brandt away from the emergency room and drove home. "You didn't see *anybody* leave the house?" he asked Brandt for the twentieth time.

"No, Dad, I swear," Brandt replied. "The front door was locked. And we would have seen somebody going through the back door."

Brandt's father drove on silently, his eyes narrowed on the road. "Perhaps I shouldn't keep such dangerous objects in the house," he murmured to himself. "But it never occurred to me that someone would actually use them."

"Dad, the ghost in the house—" Brandt started.

His father raised a hand from the wheel, a signal to stop. "Not now, Brandt. No ghost talk now."

"But, Dad, I really think—"

"Not now, Brandt. Let's talk about the ghost later. After we've both had a chance to calm down."

Brandt leaned back in his seat and shut his eyes.

He kept picturing the girls sprawled on the floor with the darts in their throats. And he kept thinking about the ghost.

The diary, he thought. Will there be a new entry in the diary? Has the ghost left another message for me?

As soon as Mr. McCloy pulled into the driveway, Brandt jumped out of the car and ran inside. He climbed straight to his room.

After making his way to the dresser, he bent to pull open the bottom drawer. Then he fumbled around in search of the diary.

Clean T-shirts, a few misplaced pairs of socks, an old letter . . .

"Hey—where'd it go?" he asked himself out loud.

The diary was gone.

He searched again. Then got to his feet.

There it was.

On the floor. By the closet. Lying open.

Brandt approached it carefully. He stood above the notebook, gazing down at it.

The diary had been opened to the last page. He could read the bold, blue writing from there.

No more Jinny or Meg.
Abbie dies next.

Chapter 25

Abbie. I've got to warn Abbie, Brandt told himself.

I've got to find her. I've got to tell her. She's in real danger. Somehow I have to make her believe me.

He started out of his room. But stopped when he reached the doorway.

There stood Abbie.

"Huh?" he cried out in shock. "You're here?" It was as if he'd conjured her up himself.

He stepped forward and grabbed her by the shoulders. "Abbie! I'm so glad you're here. Did my parents let you in?"

Abbie nodded. "Yes. What's wrong, Brandt?"

"Abbie—I—I was going to look for you. You're in terrible danger!" he blurted out.

Her features twisted in confusion. "Danger?" she repeated.

"Yes," Brandt replied breathlessly. "Abbie, you were right. This house is evil. You've got to get out of here—and never come back!"

He locked his eyes on hers, studying her face, waiting for her reaction. Would she believe him?

She *had to!*

Abbie stood perfectly still for a moment.

Then she tossed back her blond hair and laughed.

"Abbie!" Brandt cried desperately. "It's not a joke. I'm serious. You've *got* to listen to me. Jinny and Meg—two girls from school—they were nearly killed here this afternoon. And you—you could be next!"

Abbie's smile faded. Her blue eyes lit up excitedly. "Why, Brandt," she said, "you've been reading my diary, *haven't* you?"

Chapter 26

*B*randt stared at her. He opened his mouth to speak, but no sound came out. "Y-your diary?" he finally stammered.

Abbie's smile returned. "Yes, *my* diary," she replied. "I hope you found it interesting, Brandt."

Before he could reply, she began to change. Brandt stared in shock as Abbie's small body stretched, her blond hair lengthened, and her sweet face twisted with rage and hatred until it became a hideous mask of evil.

He froze in terror as a completely different person stood in front of him.

Abbie was gone.

"What I wrote in my diary has come true," the girl told him. "Abbie is dead. She was only a disguise that I wore."

Brandt still struggled to speak. But he could utter only a horrified cry.

"I am Cally," the girl announced, her cold blue eyes freezing him as she glared at him. "The ghost of Cally Frasier."

Brandt turned his eyes away. He backed against the wall, trying to steady his trembling body.

She had once been pretty, that was clear. But now her face was monstrous. Her eyes burned with cruelty, her mouth a red sneer.

He turned back in time to see her float toward him.

Brandt pressed his back against the wall. "What are you going to do to me?" he cried.

She loomed closer, her hands clasped behind her back. "Don't worry, Brandt. I won't hurt you. I care about you. Don't you know that?"

Her breath blew cold on his face as she spoke. Cold as death. Brandt shivered.

"I'm not going to hurt you, Brandt. Not really. I'm going to protect you," Cally assured him with an icy smile. "I was so lonely, Brandt. My family left me here. But then you came, and I wasn't alone anymore."

"Cally, please—" he begged.

She hovered closer, ignoring his plea. "So I'm going to keep you here with me, Brandt. Forever. Keep you here and never be lonely again."

"No, please!" Brandt pleaded. "We'll move away from here. I promise! We'll all leave tonight!" he cried desperately.

"No, Brandt, I don't think so," Cally whispered, her cold breath chilling his skin. "Your parents can leave if they want to. I don't care. But you're not going anywhere. You will be mine forever."

She brought her right hand forward. It held a small, decorated hatchet.

Brandt recognized it. It belonged to his father's collection.

Cally raised the hatchet over her head.

"No—" Brandt begged, raising his hands to shield himself. "Cally, please—"

"It will hurt for only a second," she murmured. "Then we'll be together."

She raised the hatchet as high as she could and brought it down hard.

It sank with a sickening crack into Brandt's skull.

Chapter 27

*B*randt leaned back against the wall. The hatchet remained buried in his head.

He stared back at Cally, watching her surprise.

He didn't move. He didn't fall. He didn't bleed.

Cally floated back, her cold blue eyes wide with confusion, her mouth twisted in shock. She raised both hands to her pale face. "Brandt?" she cried.

He didn't move.

"Brandt? What's happening?" she demanded in a trembling whisper.

She circled him warily, her hands still pressed to her cheeks. Her expression changed from confusion to anger. "Die!" she cried. "I killed you, Brandt! I killed you!"

Neither of them moved or spoke.

Then Brandt slowly moved his right arm.

Cally's eyes widened.

Brandt's arm reached up. He yanked the hatchet from his skull.

And tossed it to the floor.

It was his turn to smile.

As his smile widened, Cally's face clouded in anger. "What's going on here?" she demanded. "Why don't you bleed? Why aren't you dead?"

"My condition—" Brandt began.

"Condition? What condition?" she demanded impatiently.

"You can't kill me," Brandt told her. "I'm already dead!"

Chapter 28

Cally's mouth opened in an *O* of surprise. She shook her head as if trying to shake away Brandt's words. "You're lying," Cally accused him.

She reached out and squeezed his arm, pinching it tightly between her icy fingers. "You can't be dead," she insisted. "You're solid. You're not a ghost."

"No, I'm not a ghost. But I *am* dead," Brandt replied.

"How—how did you die?" Cally demanded angrily, challenging him.

Brandt bent down to pick up the hatchet. He hefted it in his hands as he spoke. "I died two years ago," he revealed.

"How?" she repeated, her eyes locked skeptically on his.

"I was poisoned," Brandt explained. "On the island of Mapolo with my parents. My father was working there, searching for rare tribal weapons."

He began to tell Cally the story, as he knew it and as his parents had told it to him. Brandt had been over and over this story in his mind, during all the nights he lay awake in bed. He kept trying to find some clue in it, or some meaning to everything that was happening to him at 99 Fear Street.

He let the hatchet fall as he began his story. "We were staying on a tiny island called Mapolo," he said. "That's where my father got those darts."

"Is that what killed you?" Cally asked suspiciously. "You were shot with a dart?"

"No," Brandt replied. "I died by mistake. Let me tell the story. Don't interrupt."

She flashed him an angry scowl, but remained silent.

"The people who live on Mapolo followed a strange religion," Brandt continued. "It involves herbs and potions, spells and rituals. They use all these things in their daily life.

"My father bought the darts from a young warrior who later thought Dad had cheated him. The warrior came to our hut one night and spread poison powder on our doorstep. Then he growled like a panther and waited for Dad to come out and see what the noise was. He assumed that my father would be the one who came out first, the one who would step into the poison powder.

"But the growling woke me up first. I went to the door and stepped outside.

"When my feet touched the powder, at first I

thought it was only sand. But then the soles of my feet began to burn. The pain was unbearable.

"I started screaming. My feet were on fire. The fire spread up my leg, all the way up through my body, until it reached my heart.

"When the poison hit my heart, I fell to the ground. I was dead. After that, all I know is what my parents told me," Brandt said. "The people in Mapolo were sorry for my parents. They put me in a coffin and they buried me."

Brandt touched the small scar on his cheek and added, "This scar was caused by one of the nails they hammered into my coffin."

Cally ran a cold hand over the scar, as if to make sure it was real.

"But my mother couldn't believe I was dead," Brandt continued. "She *wouldn't* believe it. She kept insisting there was a mistake.

"So my father went to a sorcerer in the village. He was like a witch doctor. He knew more about magic and spells than anyone else on the island. He gave people potions and medicines. He might have made the poison that killed me, for all I know.

"The sorcerer said to my parents, 'Your son's death does not have to last. He is missing only one part of his spirit—the life force. His life force has been taken away from him. But I can give him a new one.'"

Cally asked, "How?"

"The sorcerer and my father dug up my grave. They dragged my coffin to the sorcerer's hut.

"The sorcerer left the coffin in a corner of the hut. He told my mother to stay by it day and night, keeping watch. 'Don't let anyone near the body,' he said.

"Then the sorcerer went up to the main road on the island. Night was coming on. He sat by the road and watched the people wander past. Some were fishermen on their way home with the day's catch. Some were women carrying fruit back to their huts.

"Then a stranger walked by. A drifter. He stumbled down the road, ragged and dirty.

"The sorcerer beckoned to him. 'You look hungry, my friend,' the sorcerer said. 'And you look tired. I am on my way home now. Come to my hut and I will feed you. You may spend the night there if you wish.'

"The drifter probably wanted to go home with the sorcerer, but he hesitated. He knew that people on Mapolo could be dangerous.

"The sorcerer said, 'You must not sleep outdoors on Mapolo. The island is full of panthers. One of them will surely eat you before morning.'

"So the drifter went with the sorcerer. He felt he had no choice."

Brandt paused. Cally's eyes fell on the leather pouch he always wore.

"Yes, Cally," Brandt assured her, tugging on the pouch. "This pouch is coming into the story soon.

"The sorcerer brought the drifter into his hut and gave him some kind of herbal tea. The tea was heavily drugged. After a few minutes the drifter lay as still as if he were dead.

"The sorcerer told my father to open my coffin. He looked at my corpse. I had been dead for only one day. My body had not yet begun to decay."

Brandt swallowed hard. It felt strange to talk about himself this way.

"My parents watched as the sorcerer went to work. He took off the drifter's clothes and handed them to my father. He told my father to dress me in the drifter's clothes.

"Then the sorcerer cut off the drifter's hair. He clipped off his fingernails. He put the hair and the fingernail clippings into a leather pouch. This pouch."

Brandt touched the leather pouch again.

"He put the pouch around my neck. Now I wore the drifter's clothes on my body, and wore his hair and nails around my neck. Still, I was dead. The drifter lay on the floor, breathing softly.

"The sorcerer and my father lowered my body on the floor beside the drifter's. Then my parents huddled in a corner and watched the sorcerer perform a strange ceremony.

"He lit a torch and danced around my body and the drifter's body in a figure eight. He chanted something in a strange language my father had never heard before. Then he waved the torch over my corpse, passing it from the drifter's body to mine, over and over again, chanting in that weird language.

"The ceremony lasted until dawn. My father said he heard a rooster crow. At that very moment he saw the drifter shudder. The man never breathed again.

"Then my father stared at me—and saw my chest move up, then down.

"My mother screamed, she was so happy. She had seen me breathe too.

"I was alive! I had been dead—but now I was alive again! I sat up, I opened my eyes. I was alive—but the drifter was dead. The sorcerer had stolen his life force—and given it to me."

Brandt sank back. His story was finished.

Cally floated closer. "Brandt," she whispered, "this is even better than I'd hoped. You're dead but you're not. You're undead!"

She threw her arms around him. "We'll have so much fun, Brandt. You and I. We'll haunt this house together—forever!"

She brought her face close to kiss him.

But a cold cloud fell over Brandt.

He raised his eyes to it—and saw the dark shadow figure that had been chasing him.

"Who—who *are* you?" Brandt cried out.

Chapter 29

*T*he shadow loomed closer, darkening the hallway as it moved. "I've come to take back my life!" the dark figure cried.

Brandt gaped into the darkness. "You!" he uttered.

As Brandt stared at the shifting dark cloud, the figure inside it began to take shape. The image came clearer, clearer, like a camera lens focusing.

The shadows faded and fell away.

Brandt found himself staring at a man. It was impossible to tell how old he was. His hair had been shorn off until he was nearly bald. He was short and wiry. The top of his head reached only to Brandt's chin.

He wore cotton pants and a cotton shirt. The clothes hung long and loose on him, clearly too large. The sleeves of the shirt flapped over his hands. The cuffs of the pants dragged along the floor.

His tiny round black eyes gleamed dully, hard and empty. Lifeless.

A cold, sickening realization shuddered through Brandt. The shadowy figure who'd been chasing him—it wasn't Cally's ghost after all.

The shadowy figure was the spirit of the drifter from the island.

"I've come to take my life back," the drifter announced in a dry whisper, the sound of crackling dead leaves from the hole that was his mouth.

"No! Stay away from me!" Brandt cried, backing away in terror. "Please—stay away!"

With lightning quickness the man's bony hand shot out and ripped the leather pouch from Brandt's neck.

"No! Please—" Brandt protested, weaker now.

Clutching the pouch, the shadowy figure grew solid. His features grew sharper and clearer in the dim light of the hallway. His skin and eyes gave off a warm glow.

"My heart is beating!" the drifter cried joyfully. "I'm alive!"

He vanished silently down the stairs.

"Please . . ." Brandt whispered helplessly. The breath seeped out of his body. He tried to inhale, to pull air in with his lungs.

But he hadn't the strength.

"Brandt?" Cally narrowed her eyes at him. "Are you okay?"

Brandt answered with a low moan. He could feel

his tongue shrivel up. As he opened his mouth, several teeth fell out.

Glancing down, he saw his hands wrinkle. The skin turned green, curled up, then dropped off in chunks.

He watched Cally's face contort in horror at the sight of him. He watched her lips moving frantically. But he couldn't hear her words. He reached up to check his ears—and realized they had fallen off.

He saw her start to scream. But then his eyes sank back in their sockets, and he saw nothing more.

"No!" Cally screamed.

"Brandt! Don't leave me!"

Brandt's body shriveled and decomposed before her eyes. His skeleton collapsed into the floor.

Cally's wails of anger and despair echoed through the house, all through the night.

Brandt had been taken from her.

She felt as if the evil of the house had defeated her once more.

She was alone again.

Epilogue

"*T*here they go," Cally muttered to herself. "I'm being abandoned once more."

She hovered in her usual place, staring out of the attic window. A cobweb draped across the ceiling just above her face. Rats scampered across the dusty floor, searching for something to nibble on.

In the street in front of the house, Cally saw a long, black hearse. Four men moved out of the house and slowly down the driveway, shouldering a shiny dark wood coffin.

"Look," Cally said, pointing out the window. She spoke as if to a friend—but she had no friends. "There it goes. There goes Brandt's coffin."

Mr. and Mrs. McCloy followed behind the coffin in a grim procession. Mr. McCloy wore a dark suit.

Mrs. McCloy wore a black dress and a black veil. Behind the veil she sobbed, her head bowed, a handkerchief pressed to her face.

"Brandt's parents," Cally said in contempt. "I never liked them. They were so stupid. So uncaring. So self-absorbed. I'm glad they're going. I can't wait for them to leave.

"Get out of my house!" she roared at them.

Of course they couldn't hear her.

The undertaker pulled open the back of the hearse. The pallbearers lowered the heavy coffin, struggling with it, then slid it inside.

The undertaker shut the door of the hearse.

Mr. and Mrs. McCloy climbed into their car.

The undertaker sat in the front seat of the hearse. He started the motor.

A tremor of grief and fury seized Cally. "No!" she screamed. "Brandt stays here with me. Don't take him away!"

But the long, black hearse pulled silently away from the curb and rolled quickly down Fear Street and out of sight.

Cally let out a long, shrill animal wail of protest. It echoed through the empty house.

The misery on Cally's face hardened into a mask. Her icy blue eyes glittered with hate.

"I won't be alone here forever," she murmured through clenched teeth. "Someone else will move into this house.

"Sooner or later, a new victim will come."

She snickered scornfully, thinking of the evil she would do—next time.

THE SECOND HORROR

"Someone will pay for my unhappiness," she vowed.

"The next people to arrive will be sorry they ever came to 99 Fear Street."

TO BE CONTINUED . . .

About the Author

"Where do you get your ideas?"

That's the question that R. L. Stine is asked most often. "I don't know where my ideas come from," he says. "But I do know that I have a lot more scary stories in my mind that I can't wait to write."

So far, he has written nearly three dozen mysteries and thrillers for young people, all of them bestsellers.

Bob grew up in Columbus, Ohio. Today he lives in an apartment near Central Park in New York City with his wife, Jane, and fourteen-year-old son, Matt.

THE NIGHTMARES NEVER END . . . WHEN YOU VISIT

Next . . .
99 FEAR STREET:
The Third Horror
(Coming in October 1994)

It's been two years since Kody Frasier left the house at 99 Fear Street. Since the evil in the house destroyed her family. And now Kody is back to star in a movie based on those horrors.

But that's not the only reason Kody has returned. When she left, she made a promise to her dead sister, Cally, that she would be back to free her from the evil. And Cally's ghost has been waiting for her.

Filming begins—and so does the terror. As the accidents grow worse and worse, Kody realizes that the evil is still at work. Does she have the power to conquer it? Or will the spirit of her own sister destroy her?